The Poisoned Chalice

Calvin Hill

Published by Calvin Hill, 2024.

This is a work of fiction. Similarities to real people, places, or events are entirely coincidental.

THE POISONED CHALICE

First edition. November 4, 2024.

Copyright © 2024 Calvin Hill.

ISBN: 979-8227147844

Written by Calvin Hill.

The Poisoned Chalice
During a medieval reenactment, a participant is poisoned, and the detective must uncover the secrets of the reenactors to find the murderer.

In the shadow of towering stone walls, banners snap in the wind, bearing crests that harken back to an era of kings, queens, and knights sworn to honour. The annual medieval reenactment at Langford Castle is in full swing, with participants donning armour, cloaks, and even powdered wigs, each carefully crafting their role in this meticulously staged spectacle. For one long weekend, the modern world falls away, replaced by the echoes of courtly intrigue, chivalric vows, and whispered promises.

But amid the revelry, darkness stirs. When the evening feast reaches its zenith, a toast rings out, chalices raised high, brimming with mead and wine. Laughter fills the hall, but only for a moment. One of the revellers stumbles, a look of terror flickering in his eyes, and collapses to the stone floor. By the time the others rush to his side, he is gone, his final breath stolen by the very cup he raised.

Detective Elise Morrigan arrives on scene, an outsider in every sense. She doesn't understand this world of role-playing nobles, warriors, and rogues, nor the layers of history and rivalries embedded in their roles. Yet, beneath the gilded armour and satin gowns, she senses something darker. These reenactors are more than dedicated hobbyists; they are bound by something deeper, something they don't want her to see.

In this world where fantasy and reality twist together, secrets linger in every whispered aside and stolen glance. Morrigan must peel back layers of deception and ambition, finding her way through a labyrinth of centuries-old grudges and new vendettas. But as she unearths one truth after another, one question haunts her: How much of this game is mere play-acting? And how much of it is real?

As the walls of Langford Castle close in, Detective Morrigan realizes that she isn't just hunting a killer—she's stepping into a treacherous world where everyone has something to hide, and no one is exactly who they seem. In The Poisoned Chalice, the line between role and reality blurs, and trust is as rare as a knight's honour.

Chapter one The Gathering Storm

The annual reenactment at Langford Castle was a spectacle that drew participants from far and wide, each eager to play their chosen roles. For one weekend each year, the castle grounds transformed into a vivid portrayal of medieval life, with banners unfurled and tents erected across the field. The air buzzed with the energy of hundreds who had taken on roles ranging from lowly peasants to gallant knights, each costume painstakingly detailed to capture the essence of a bygone era.

At the heart of the reenactment was the evening feast—a lavish celebration held in the Great Hall of Langford Castle. As dawn broke on the first day of festivities, participants were already in character, weaving in and out of roles with varying degrees of commitment. Some embraced their medieval identities with solemn intensity, while others approached it as a light-hearted game.

One of the first to arrive on the castle grounds that morning was Lord Edwin St. Clair, a self-assured man who had spent the better part of the last decade refining his role as the lord of Langford. In costume, he wore a tunic adorned with a stylized hawk crest, marking his self-appointed status as the "overseer" of the event. Edwin took this responsibility seriously, ensuring that every aspect of the reenactment met his exacting standards. For Edwin, the weekend was not merely a hobby; it was a tradition he upheld with reverence.

Then there was Lady Isolde Whitford, a formidable woman who claimed the role of Lady of the Manor, second only to Edwin's in the social hierarchy of the reenactment. Lady Isolde's character was known for her poise and sharp wit, and she rarely broke from it, even when speaking to others outside of the reenactment setting. Draped in a gown of deep emerald velvet, with intricate embroidery lining the sleeves, she was every inch a medieval noblewoman. She had cultivated her position as Edwin's rival in the reenactment, a role that suited her both on and off the field.

Elsewhere, setting up tents and arranging props, were Sir Gareth and his squire, Elias. Sir Gareth was a brooding figure, a role enhanced by his imposing armour and the calculated intensity with which he moved. Gareth prided himself on his knowledge of medieval combat and often took on the role of training others in swordsmanship. To him, the reenactment was an exercise in discipline, a means of connecting with a past he admired. His squire, Elias, was younger and far less sure of himself, often fumbling with the heavy equipment. But despite his clumsiness, Elias seemed devoted to his duties, never questioning Gareth's commands.

Closer to the castle's entrance, Lady Eleanor Addington mingled with other participants, her laughter bright and infectious. Eleanor, in her elaborate headdress and silk gown, had a knack for diplomacy and was often the one to settle minor disputes among the participants. As one of the event's most longstanding members, she was familiar with everyone and always managed to appear neutral, though in truth, she was often privy to the undercurrents of tension that flowed beneath the surface.

The castle's courtyard, meanwhile, was a bustling center of activity. Vendors selling handcrafted goods, blacksmiths demonstrating medieval techniques, and children dressed as young squires or apprentices added to the atmosphere. Musicians played flutes and lutes, adding a layer of authenticity to the gathering, their melodies drifting on the morning breeze. The reenactors moved among the crowd with an air of purpose, addressing one another by titles and maintaining their chosen roles with varying degrees of seriousness.

Despite the camaraderie, small tensions simmered among the participants. Over the years, a series of unspoken rivalries had developed, with certain individuals vying for higher status within the group. At the top of this informal hierarchy stood Edwin and Isolde, but there were others who aspired to more influential roles. Sir Gareth, for example, often argued with Edwin over the allocation of resources

THE POISONED CHALICE   5

and the distribution of titles, believing that Edwin played favourites when it came to promoting those who displayed the most "authenticity."

As the morning continued, these tensions grew less hidden. A small disagreement broke out near the armoury tent, where Gareth and Edwin engaged in a terse exchange over the proper arrangement of weapons. "A knight's arsenal should reflect the nobility of his purpose," Gareth argued, holding up a broadsword with the grip of a man who had long practiced his craft. Edwin, however, dismissed him with a practiced smile. "And yet, you forget, Sir Gareth, that these are props. We must balance historical accuracy with practicality," he replied smoothly, moving on before Gareth could respond.

Nearby, Lady Isolde watched the interaction with a barely concealed smirk. She had no love for Gareth and frequently took Edwin's side in these matters, finding satisfaction in seeing Gareth's ambitions thwarted. Isolde's own rivalries, however, were not confined to Gareth. She held her own grudge against Lady Eleanor, whom she saw as overly sympathetic and a little too eager to play the peacekeeper. Isolde prided herself on her knowledge of history and tradition, believing that Eleanor's diplomatic approach watered down the seriousness of the reenactment.

The younger participants, like Elias and a few others acting as squires or junior members of the reenactment, often felt caught in the middle of these feuds. They were tasked with following orders, but loyalties were rarely straightforward. Elias, for example, admired Gareth's commitment to authenticity but felt the weight of Edwin's authority. He, like many others, walked a fine line, careful not to anger anyone in the process.

As the day unfolded, reenactors gathered for the opening ceremony, a formal procession from the castle gates to the inner courtyard. The procession was led by Edwin and Isolde, who walked side by side, each playing their roles to perfection. Following them were knights, ladies, and courtiers in full regalia, their robes and armour glinting under the midday sun. This parade of characters moved in a stately fashion, the crowd applauding as they passed. Children gasped, while adults watched with appreciation, some nodding in approval of the authenticity displayed in the costumes and demeanour of the participants.

Once the opening ceremony concluded, the day's activities began in earnest. A staged tournament was set up in the courtyard, with knights preparing for mock duels and jousting matches. Gareth, eager to showcase his swordsmanship, took on a younger knight in a duel that drew a large audience. His movements were precise and intense, each swing and parry executed with a level of skill that few could match. As he fought, he cast a glance toward Edwin, who watched from the sidelines, unimpressed.

Elsewhere, Lady Eleanor led a storytelling session for children, recounting tales of chivalry and bravery in a gentle tone. She laughed easily, enchanting her young audience, who hung on her every word. Eleanor's role as the castle's "noble heart" was well-established, and she excelled in engaging the crowd, drawing them into the atmosphere of the medieval world they had come to experience.

As the afternoon wore on, the reenactment grew livelier. A minstrels' performance attracted a large crowd, their music setting a joyful mood as people mingled, laughed, and spoke of the evening feast, eagerly anticipated as the highlight of the day. Rumours of the planned menu spread, with mentions of roasted boar, fresh-baked bread, and an array of fine meads that would fill the Great Hall with the ambiance of an ancient banquet.

Yet, beneath the outward merriment, those involved knew there was more to the evening than just feasting. The event held deeper meaning for many, serving as a stage not only for play-acting but for asserting status, venting frustrations, and settling scores. For some, like Edwin and Isolde, it was a matter of pride. For others, like Gareth,

THE POISONED CHALICE 7

it was a chance to gain recognition, perhaps even to challenge the established order.

As the sun dipped lower, casting a golden glow over Langford Castle, the participants prepared for the grand banquet in the Great Hall. Each donned their finest costumes, checking the details one last time. The atmosphere grew tense, with rivalries momentarily put aside in favour of a shared commitment to spectacle. The feast would begin soon, and everyone knew that the toast—a tradition held in honour of the reenactment's opening night—would be the culmination of their efforts and anticipation.

As they gathered in the Great Hall, candles flickered against the stone walls, casting long shadows across the tables laden with food. The sound of goblets clinking and laughter echoed through the hall, but for some, the evening's festivities were more than an exercise in medieval play; they were an opportunity. Secrets were guarded closely, and glances were exchanged as each prepared to raise their chalice.

Unbeknownst to the revellers, a storm was brewing just beneath the surface, one that would change the course of this year's reenactment—and of several lives—forever.

Chapter 2 – The Cast Assemble

The rain had just started to drizzle as Detective Elise Morrigan drove through the winding roads leading up to Langford Castle. She peered through her windshield, eyeing the dark silhouette of the castle against a backdrop of grey clouds, wondering what she'd signed herself up for.

Her hands gripped the steering wheel a little tighter than usual. This wasn't her usual sort of case; she was used to dealing with straightforward crime scenes, not elaborate fantasy role-plays where the lines between reality and performance blurred. Elise had heard of the annual reenactment weekend at Langford, of course—who hadn't in this part of the county? But she'd never expected to be a part of it, and certainly not as the only person there who didn't seem to belong.

As she parked her car just outside the castle grounds, Elise took a deep breath and stepped out, shrugging on her raincoat. She was an outsider, and she knew it. Aware of how people in insular communities could close ranks, especially ones as invested in their shared fantasy as these reenactors, she prepared herself for a mix of fascination and hostility.

Elise began her walk toward the castle entrance, taking in the scene around her. The courtyard was alive with activity, bustling with characters from another era. There were knights clad in shining armour, ladies draped in velvet gowns, and townsfolk in simple tunics, all milling about with an intensity of purpose that left her intrigued. The faint strains of a lute echoed across the courtyard, and Elise caught the smell of roasting meat wafting from a nearby tent.

She found herself surrounded by a medieval marketplace of sorts. Blacksmiths hammered away at metal, merchants sold trinkets and handmade crafts, and children ran through the crowd, playing knights and squires. Though she wasn't one to admit it easily, she could see the appeal of such a vivid escape. The world here seemed tangible yet carefully crafted, almost real enough to believe in.

THE POISONED CHALICE

As she approached the castle gates, a figure caught her eye—a man clad in meticulously maintained armour, every piece polished to a reflective sheen. He moved through the courtyard like he owned it, nodding curtly at passersby who greeted him. Sir Gareth, she remembered from her briefing notes. The "brooding knight," as the locals called him, known for his intensity and strict adherence to the "rules" of the reenactment. His reputation preceded him: a skilled fighter with a dark edge, one who took his role a bit too seriously for many people's tastes.

Elise watched as he spoke sternly to a young man beside him, presumably his squire. The young man's head was bowed, his face tense with concentration, as Gareth instructed him on how to properly carry a shield. She observed the way Gareth held himself, the weight of his authority palpable. He was more than just a man in costume; he was someone who lived his role.

Moving past Gareth, Elise's eyes fell on a small group gathered near the armoury tent. At the center was Lady Isolde, her dark hair falling in soft waves over a richly embroidered cloak. There was a calculated elegance to her movements, and Elise could tell at a glance that she was used to being the center of attention. Isolde's expression was sharp, her gaze hawk-like as she watched the interactions around her with a cool detachment.

Just then, Lady Isolde's gaze met Elise's for a brief moment, and the look she received was one of undisguised assessment. Elise couldn't help but feel like she was being sized up, as if she were a potential rival in a world where alliances were vital and grudges long-lasting. Elise had read about Isolde's rivalry with Gareth and Edwin; though supposedly friendly, their tension had become something of a legend among the reenactors. Elise imagined that years of shared history and competition had layered their interactions with more than a hint of resentment.

A rustling sound to her left made Elise turn, and she saw Edwin St. Clair emerging from the armoury tent, flanked by a few other costumed participants. His presence was imposing, his demeanour both dignified and aloof. As the "lord" of the reenactment, Edwin had taken on the role of overseeing the entire event. In his burgundy robe trimmed with gold, he looked every bit the medieval nobleman, complete with a crest pinned to his chest that identified him as the lord of Langford. He exchanged polite nods with those around him, keeping his expression neutral.

Elise watched as Edwin spoke with Lady Eleanor, another prominent figure in the reenactment. Eleanor was dressed in soft lavender, her gown flowing around her like water as she gestured animatedly, her face a picture of kindness and warmth. Eleanor's laughter echoed across the courtyard, and she seemed to draw people to her with ease. Unlike Isolde, whose interactions seemed shrouded in tension, Eleanor's charm was effortless. She was beloved by the group, known for her diplomatic nature and her ability to keep the peace. Elise made a mental note of her—she sensed Eleanor's popularity could be both an asset and a liability in a group like this.

Continuing her way through the courtyard, Elise caught sight of a few younger participants, barely out of their teens, dressed as squires and minor characters. They flitted around, carrying equipment and supplies, often stopping to speak in hushed voices. She overheard snippets of their conversations, many filled with excitement about the upcoming feast. Their wide-eyed enthusiasm was a stark contrast to the older, more serious participants, who seemed to carry a burden of unspoken grievances and past conflicts.

Just then, a shrill laugh drew her attention to a merchant's booth where a large man with a booming voice was hawking "medieval" wares—most likely cheap replicas, but convincing enough to blend into the scene. The man grinned broadly, waving a flagon of ale in one hand while entertaining a small group. He introduced himself as Otto the Bold, a minor character but clearly a favorite among the visitors. His easy-going nature and loud, jovial personality made him hard to miss.

THE POISONED CHALICE 11

Elise couldn't help but smile as he winked at her, seemingly unaware that she was anything other than another curious visitor.

She moved onward, pausing to study each figure she passed. It was an odd sensation, Elise thought, to be surrounded by so many people who had, for all intents and purposes, left their real identities behind. Their commitment to their roles was complete, and she wondered what drove each of them to such dedication. Some, like Eleanor, seemed to thrive in the camaraderie and theatricality. Others, like Gareth, seemed almost haunted by their roles, as if they'd invested so much of themselves that they no longer saw where the act ended and they began.

A quiet voice interrupted her thoughts. "New to the court, are we?"

Elise turned to see an elderly woman, her face lined with years, standing beside her. The woman's simple clothing marked her as a villager, yet her eyes sparkled with intelligence. "I'm Margaret," she said, bowing her head slightly, "keeper of the stories, so to speak."

Elise raised an eyebrow, intrigued. "Keeper of the stories?"

Margaret chuckled softly. "Every court needs its chronicler. I keep track of the tales, you might say. Every rivalry, every old grudge, every friendship born and broken." Her eyes held a hint of mischief. "And believe me, there are plenty to keep track of here."

"I imagine you must know a great deal about everyone," Elise replied, glancing back at Gareth, who was now speaking animatedly to his squire.

"Oh, indeed. Each one of them has their secrets," Margaret replied, her voice barely above a whisper. "Some hide them well. Others... not so much."

Before Elise could probe further, Margaret gave her a knowing smile and slipped back into the crowd, leaving her with a sense of quiet unease.

She felt the weight of her task settle on her shoulders. These people weren't just weekend hobbyists. They had invested themselves in these roles so deeply that the lines between their personas and their real selves were blurred, if not entirely erased. Each of them, she sensed, wore their costume like a second skin, a shield against the outside world—and, perhaps, against their own darker impulses.

As Elise made her way through the last of the tents and prepared to enter the Great Hall, she glanced back at the courtyard, now cast in the muted tones of a grey afternoon. She watched as the reenactors laughed, whispered, and moved about in their carefully crafted roles, all seemingly oblivious to her presence. Yet she felt their eyes on her, their curiosity hidden beneath their masks.

She realized, with a chill, that beneath the pageantry and medieval charm, this was not a friendly gathering. She could sense it in the hushed conversations, in the way some participants avoided each other's eyes, in the way rivalries simmered just beneath the surface. She was stepping into a world of hidden agendas and tangled histories.

And she couldn't shake the feeling that, somehow, these secrets would eventually catch up with them all.

Chapter 3: The Last Draught

The Great Hall of Langford Castle was a marvel to behold. Tables laden with roasted meats, freshly baked breads, and goblets of spiced wine stretched the length of the room, a feast fit for kings and queens. Tapestries hung along the stone walls, their intricate patterns catching the flicker of candlelight. The hall was alive with laughter and the clinking of goblets, as the reenactors immersed themselves fully in the spirit of the evening. For a few hours, the modern world had slipped away entirely, leaving only the illusion of medieval grandeur.

At the head of the main table sat Edwin St. Clair, in his role as lord of the castle, flanked by Lady Isolde and Lady Eleanor. They shared a polite, if strained, camaraderie. Edwin, draped in a deep burgundy robe with a fur-lined collar, raised his goblet to greet the guests who approached him, all part of his nobleman's persona. To his left, Lady Isolde sat in her emerald gown, her gaze sharp as she surveyed the room. She exchanged pleasantries but rarely allowed her guard to drop, her expression hinting at both amusement and disdain. Eleanor, meanwhile, played her role with an air of effortless grace, laughing and chatting with those who passed her, always warm and inviting.

Down the table, Sir Gareth was laughing boisterously, his voice echoing above the general chatter. In character as always, he leaned into his role as a knight, recounting tales of bravery to the younger participants seated nearby, who listened with wide eyes. His squire, Elias, sat beside him, eyes darting nervously between Gareth and the feast, clearly anxious about maintaining his lord's high expectations. Gareth lifted his goblet repeatedly, toasting each tale with a hearty swig of wine, while his audience responded with polite, awed applause.

The atmosphere grew livelier as the evening wore on. Musicians at the far end of the hall struck up a melody, adding a rhythmic backdrop to the revelry. People clinked goblets, laughed, and shared whispered conversations. Elise Morrigan, seated unobtrusively near the back, observed it all with a quiet intensity. Her gaze drifted from one guest to the next, cataloguing each face, noting the subtle gestures and hidden glances. She could see the layers of intrigue beneath the cheerful surface, sensing the unspoken tensions that lingered in the air.

As the musicians' tune slowed, Edwin rose to his feet, goblet in hand. The hall quieted in a wave, all eyes turning toward him. Edwin's expression was solemn, his gaze sweeping over the crowd.

"Friends, guests, noble lords and ladies," he began, his voice carrying through the hall with practiced authority, "tonight we celebrate more than our shared love of history. We celebrate loyalty, courage, and tradition. This feast honours the chivalry of old, the bravery of our forebears." His words, though rehearsed, were met with nods of approval and a few scattered murmurs of agreement.

Edwin lifted his goblet higher, signalling the group to do the same. The room collectively raised their cups, the clinking of glass filling the hall. "To the old ways," Edwin declared, his voice echoing off the stone walls, "and to the bonds of honour we forge tonight!"

As the crowd echoed his words, their voices a rumbling chorus, Elise felt a chill skitter down her spine. Something about the unity of it, the old words spoken with such conviction, seemed almost ritualistic. She glanced over at Gareth, who met her gaze for a brief, unreadable moment before lifting his chalice with a slight smirk.

"To the old ways!" Gareth repeated, louder than the rest, his eyes flashing as he drank deeply from his goblet. His followers at the table followed suit, lifting their own cups in earnest, their loyalty to him palpable even in play.

The moment was brief but electric, a rare moment of shared fervour. Then, as the laughter resumed and the guests lowered their goblets, Gareth's expression changed. His face paled, his confident smirk slipping into something more akin to confusion. Elise noticed it first—the way his hand trembled as he tried to steady his goblet,

THE POISONED CHALICE 15

his eyes widening as though he were struggling to make sense of some unseen horror.

Gareth's fingers loosened, and the goblet slipped from his grip, clattering onto the table and spilling wine across the polished wood. He clutched his throat, his breaths coming shallow and quick, eyes darting around the room in a mixture of panic and disbelief. A faint gasp rippled through the crowd as those closest to him realized something was terribly wrong.

Lady Isolde was the first to react, her expression shifting from casual indifference to alarm. "Gareth?" she asked, her tone sharp with concern, but he didn't respond. His face was turning an alarming shade of grey, and he made a guttural choking sound, collapsing forward, his body sprawling across the table.

Elise was on her feet before she'd fully registered her own movement, instinct taking over. She moved quickly through the crowd, the sounds of gasps and whispers barely registering in her mind as she reached Gareth's side. His breathing was shallow, his lips tinged blue, and his eyes were glazed with a look of sheer terror.

"Someone call for help!" Elise shouted, her voice cutting through the growing commotion. But deep down, she knew it was already too late.

Lady Eleanor, standing nearby, covered her mouth with a trembling hand, her eyes wide with horror. Edwin, for once speechless, looked on in shock as Gareth's body went limp, his breathing slowing until, finally, he lay still. The room fell into a deathly silence, the joyous ambiance shattered beyond repair.

Elise felt her heart hammer in her chest as she straightened, turning to face the stunned assembly. Her eyes swept the room, taking in the pale, horrified faces of the reenactors. Some looked away, others stared at Gareth's body, and a few exchanged uneasy glances.

Edwin, visibly shaken, managed to speak, his voice a broken murmur. "How... how could this happen?" he stammered, his gaze locked on Gareth's lifeless form. "It was only... it was only a game..."

Elise felt a surge of frustration rise within her. She'd sensed something was off from the moment she'd arrived at Langford, but she hadn't anticipated this. What had started as a harmless reenactment had turned into something far darker.

"Poison," she murmured, more to herself than to anyone else, examining the goblet Gareth had dropped. It still lay on its side, a dark smear of wine staining the table. She leaned in, her mind working quickly, recalling her brief lessons in toxicology. The bluish tint to his lips, the sudden collapse—all pointed to a fast-acting poison.

Across the table, Lady Isolde looked at her, horror mingling with something else in her expression—a strange intensity that Elise couldn't quite place. "Who would... who could do such a thing?" she whispered, her voice barely audible.

Elise met Isolde's gaze, holding it for a moment longer than necessary. "That's what I intend to find out."

The crowd began to stir, murmurs growing louder as the shock wore off and panic set in. Elise stepped back, her mind racing. This was no accident, and she couldn't ignore the unsettling possibility that someone in this room had carefully planned Gareth's death. Perhaps they had even seen his poisoning as part of the reenactment—a dark twist in their medieval drama.

"Everyone," Edwin's voice trembled but managed a semblance of control, "please, return to your quarters. I'll... I'll arrange for Gareth to be taken care of. This is a terrible tragedy."

A murmur of agreement rose from the crowd, though Elise noted that no one moved, their feet rooted to the floor in shock. She watched as Lady Eleanor placed a trembling hand on Edwin's shoulder, whispering something to him before he nodded and began ushering the guests away, his usual confidence replaced by a numb resignation.

THE POISONED CHALICE   17

Elise lingered, watching the reenactors file out, each person's face a mask of shock, confusion, or, in some cases, suspicion. She observed Isolde's quick, almost furtive glance at Gareth's body before she hurried from the room. Eleanor, her face pale, clutched the arm of a fellow participant, her expression a mixture of horror and sadness.

As the last of the guests left the Great Hall, Elise turned her attention back to Gareth's goblet. She pulled on a pair of gloves from her coat pocket and carefully examined the rim, her gaze narrowing at the faint residue clinging to it. It wasn't enough for her to identify the poison outright, but it confirmed her suspicions.

The flickering candlelight cast long shadows across the empty hall, illuminating the remnants of the feast—the plates left half-eaten, the spilled wine pooling on the table. She let out a slow breath, the silence of the hall now deafening.

The poison had been expertly administered. It wasn't a careless act but one that required forethought and a precise understanding of its effects. Whoever had done this knew Gareth well enough to anticipate his behaviour, his habits. They knew he would drink deeply when toasting the "old ways," knew he would trust that his goblet was safe.

This was no accident. It was an execution, a calculated act that had been waiting for the right moment.

Elise stood alone in the hall, the weight of the situation pressing down on her. She had a murder on her hands, and this case would be anything but simple. In a gathering of people who lived half in a fantasy and half in reality, where grudges and ambitions ran deep, the truth would be buried beneath layers of performance and deception.

And with every clue she uncovered, she knew one thing for certain: she was stepping into a world far darker than she had anticipated.

Chapter 4: The First Glance

The Great Hall felt colder than it had only moments ago. The flickering candlelight did little to dispel the heavy silence that had settled over the room like a shroud. Elise Morrigan took a slow breath, gathering herself as she moved closer to Sir Gareth's lifeless body, her sharp gaze assessing every detail with practiced intensity.

The reenactors clustered together, their faces pale, eyes wide with disbelief, watching Elise with a mixture of fear and curiosity. She could feel their eyes on her, but her focus remained on Gareth, who lay slumped across the table. His hand, which had once gripped his goblet with such bravado, was now curled lifelessly against the wood, fingers frozen in a twisted grasp.

After a quick, preliminary examination of the scene, Elise straightened, finally allowing herself to look up and take in the faces of those around her. She saw more than just shock in their eyes; there was an intensity—a sense of shared guilt or guarded secrets—that lingered in each expression. These people were not mere bystanders to a tragedy; they were participants in something intricate and entangled, something dark.

Lady Isolde was standing near the end of the table, her emerald gown brushing the floor as she stared down at Gareth with an inscrutable expression. Her face was pale, yet her eyes burned with an intensity that Elise found unsettling. There was shock there, certainly, but layered beneath it was something that looked almost like satisfaction—or perhaps relief. Elise's gaze lingered on her, curious. Was Isolde hiding a sense of victory beneath her grief?

Beside Isolde, Edwin St. Clair seemed visibly shaken, though he attempted to maintain a façade of authority. His hands were clasped tightly in front of him, and he had the look of someone trying to mask his emotions behind a wall of forced composure. But Edwin's eyes betrayed him; they darted nervously between Gareth's body and the

THE POISONED CHALICE

onlookers. Elise noted how he avoided meeting anyone's gaze directly, as if fearful that his own emotions might spill over.

Edwin and Gareth had been rivals, according to her briefing. Their disputes were well-known among the group, and though they'd always managed to keep their clashes "in character," she could sense that there was more animosity beneath the surface than mere rivalry. Edwin's expression, taut and uneasy, hinted at a kind of helplessness he wasn't accustomed to.

To Edwin's right, Lady Eleanor held a delicate hand to her mouth, her fingers trembling slightly. Unlike the others, Eleanor's face displayed genuine grief, her eyes glistening as she looked down at Gareth. She seemed almost dazed, as if struggling to process the horror that had unfolded before her. Elise watched her closely, noting the way Eleanor clutched her gown, her knuckles white. Eleanor's grief appeared real, but Elise couldn't ignore the flicker of fear that passed over her face as she glanced at the others. Did she fear for herself or for someone else?

At the far side of the table, Otto the Bold, the jovial merchant, stood apart from the others. His face was a mask of confusion, and his eyes darted around the room, his brow furrowing as he took in the reactions of his companions. Unlike the more sombre figures around him, Otto appeared out of place in his distress, as if he'd stumbled into a drama he wasn't prepared for. He mumbled something to himself, looking down at his own goblet as if wondering whether it, too, might hold a deadly secret.

Elise's gaze moved down the table, where Gareth's squire, Elias, was clutching the back of a chair, his face ashen. He looked utterly horrified, his youthful confidence shattered, and his hands trembled as he held onto the wood with a white-knuckled grip. There was a glint of guilt in his eyes, mingled with raw fear. Elias's admiration for Gareth had been obvious; the young squire had always looked up to the knight with awe. Now, that awe had curdled into terror. Elise noted how Elias kept his head down, his gaze averted, as if fearing he might be accused simply by association.

As Elise moved down the length of the table, she caught snippets of hurried, whispered conversations among the reenactors, their voices trembling with fear and suspicion.

"Who would do such a thing?" one woman murmured, clutching her goblet tightly, her gaze darting between the faces around her.

"Someone must have tampered with the wine," a man whispered, his face pale. "It was the chalice; I saw him drink from it!"

The more Elise observed, the clearer it became that this was not merely a reenactment gone wrong; there was a complex web of relationships, rivalries, and resentments that bound these people together. And each of them seemed to wear their emotions with a slight edge, as though each interaction hid a concealed dagger.

Lady Isolde's voice cut through the murmurs, sharp and cool. "Enough," she said, her voice carrying across the hall. She stepped forward, addressing the crowd with an air of command. "Whatever happened here was deliberate. This was no accident."

Her words settled over the group like a curse. Eyes widened, and Elise noted how a few of the reenactors recoiled slightly, as though realizing, perhaps for the first time, the gravity of what had happened. Isolde's expression was stern, her gaze hard as she looked over the assembly. It was clear that, if given the opportunity, she would step into Edwin's role as leader without hesitation.

Edwin's jaw tightened at Isolde's assertion, and he raised his hands in an attempt to regain control. "Let's not jump to conclusions, Lady Isolde," he said, his tone clipped. "We don't know what happened yet."

But Isolde's words had already taken root. The group shifted uneasily, some casting nervous glances at the door as if they might flee. Elise saw fear, suspicion, and something else: the dawning realization that the game had become deadly serious.

THE POISONED CHALICE

21

She stepped forward, her voice firm. "I'm Detective Elise Morrigan. I know this is a shock, but I need everyone to stay calm and stay here." Her words cut through the panic, and silence fell as the group turned their attention to her. "I'll be conducting a thorough investigation, but I need your cooperation. No one leaves the hall until we have some answers."

The reenactors looked at her with a mixture of relief and resentment. This wasn't the kind of role they'd imagined her playing, nor was it one she'd expected. But in that moment, Elise saw a shift, a reluctant acceptance of her authority, even if it came with a touch of disdain from those who'd preferred her to stay an outsider.

Isolde's eyes narrowed, a hint of challenge in her gaze. "And what exactly do you plan to do, Detective?" Her tone was polite, but Elise could feel the edge to her words, a subtle reminder that Elise was an intruder in their world.

Elise held her gaze, unflinching. "I plan to find out who killed Sir Gareth," she replied. "And I suggest you start considering what you know, what you've seen, and what you might be hiding. Because every one of you will be answering questions."

Lady Eleanor, still visibly shaken, spoke up. "But who would want to hurt Gareth?" Her voice was a soft whisper, laden with genuine sorrow. "He was... he was one of us."

Elise looked at Eleanor, seeing the pain etched in her features. But her question felt rhetorical, almost naïve, given what Elise had already observed. Clearly, Eleanor had either been ignorant of Gareth's conflicts or preferred to ignore them. And yet, Elise couldn't help but feel that Eleanor's innocence was genuine.

At the far end of the hall, Elias suddenly choked back a sob, his hands trembling as he stepped forward. "He... he was a good knight. He didn't deserve..." His words trailed off as his eyes met Elise's, wide with fear. "Detective, please—you have to believe me. I would never..."

Elise raised a calming hand. "We'll talk soon, Elias. I need you to take a few deep breaths."

Elias nodded, though his expression remained haunted, guilt simmering behind his gaze.

As Elise took a final glance around the room, she felt the weight of what lay ahead. Every face was a mask, every gaze a story waiting to be uncovered. Behind each pair of eyes, secrets festered, some ancient, others perhaps as fresh as the wine spilled across the table. And while they might have viewed Gareth's death as a shock, there were some who barely concealed their indifference—or, in Isolde's case, perhaps a dark satisfaction.

Elise realized that finding the truth would mean peeling back these layers, unmasking not only Gareth's killer but each person in this room who had contributed to the poisoned atmosphere that lingered like a shadow over the castle.

The first glance had revealed much, but Elise knew it was only the beginning.

Chapter 5: Roles and Rivalries

Elise sat in a small antechamber off the Great Hall, its stone walls cold and foreboding. The castle staff had hastily arranged a table and chair for her, where she would conduct the interviews. She took a moment to steady herself, mentally preparing for what promised to be a long night. The participants' faces, their tense expressions, flashed through her mind as she shuffled through her notes. This group wasn't just here to play dress-up—they were deeply invested in their characters, and that made everything more complicated.

Lady Isolde was her first interview. Elise had chosen her deliberately, sensing that the woman knew more than she let on. Isolde entered the room with her usual poise, her emerald gown sweeping along the stone floor as she took the seat opposite Elise, folding her hands neatly in her lap. Her expression was calm, controlled, almost bored, as if this were a mere formality.

"Lady Isolde," Elise began, "or perhaps I should call you by your real name—Clara Whitford."

Isolde's lips curved into a faint smile. "You may call me Clara, but for the purposes of our discussion, I'll remain Lady Isolde. It's the role I'm comfortable with, Detective, and as you'll find, these roles mean a great deal to us."

"Clearly," Elise replied, her tone even. "Tell me, what is the nature of your role here?"

Isolde's smile sharpened. "I am Lady of the Manor, second only to Lord Edwin in this little medieval kingdom we've created. My role is to uphold the traditions of court, to ensure that our proceedings remain in line with history—and, yes, occasionally to keep others in check. There's a certain level of authority that comes with the title."

"And Gareth?" Elise prompted. "What was his role, and how did it relate to yours?"

Isolde's expression darkened. "Sir Gareth was... an ambitious knight, to say the least. He was a loud voice in our group, always advocating for a stricter adherence to authenticity. He fancied himself the castle's chief warrior, the most noble of us all." She paused, her eyes narrowing slightly. "But he was also difficult. Prone to challenging authority, especially Edwin's. And mine."

"So you clashed," Elise noted.

"Certainly," Isolde replied with a dismissive wave. "He and I had... disagreements. Gareth's vision for the group often conflicted with mine. He thought I was too concerned with appearances, that I didn't understand the 'true' spirit of our little court. But he was wrong. I know the history as well as he did; I simply chose to interpret it differently."

Elise raised an eyebrow. "It sounds like you didn't get along."

"Getting along is irrelevant here, Detective," Isolde replied, her voice sharp. "It's about respect. Gareth and I disagreed, yes, but we respected each other's positions. He was a knight, and I am Lady of the Manor. Disputes were... part of the game."

Elise nodded thoughtfully. "And what about Edwin? Did Gareth respect him?"

Isolde's gaze flickered, a hint of something unsaid lingering in her eyes. "Edwin is... respected, yes. But not by all. Gareth often accused him of being more interested in playing lord than in maintaining authenticity. Gareth was... outspoken about it."

"Would you say Gareth saw himself as Edwin's rival?"

Isolde tilted her head, considering the question. "In some ways, yes. But he also respected the hierarchy. Despite his arrogance, he wouldn't have openly undermined Edwin's role."

Elise watched her carefully, noting the quick shifts in her expressions. It was clear that Isolde had spent years navigating these power dynamics, and while she was composed, there was an edge to her voice that hinted at deeper grievances.

THE POISONED CHALICE

"Thank you, Lady Isolde," Elise said finally. "That will be all for now."

Isolde rose gracefully, giving Elise a slight nod before gliding out of the room, leaving behind a lingering tension. As Elise prepared for her next interview, she reflected on Isolde's words. The rivalry with Gareth was evident, but there was a sense of cold detachment in her answers, as though she wanted to distance herself from Gareth's death.

The door opened again, and Edwin St. Clair entered. He looked weary, his usual air of authority dampened by the events of the evening. He sat down with a sigh, running a hand through his carefully styled hair.

"Elise Morrigan, isn't it?" he began, offering a strained smile. "Thank you for agreeing to take on this... unpleasant task."

"Let's start with your role here, Edwin," Elise said, diving straight into her questions. "I understand you're the lord of this reenactment group."

"Yes, that's correct," he replied, nodding. "As 'Lord Edwin,' I oversee the entire court. It's my responsibility to make sure everyone adheres to their roles, maintains respect for the historical aspect of our activities. I coordinate the reenactments, allocate roles, settle disputes when they arise."

"Disputes?" Elise prompted. "Can you elaborate on that?"

Edwin hesitated, his fingers tapping nervously on the table. "In a group like ours, Detective, people take their roles seriously—sometimes too seriously. Rivalries develop, misunderstandings occur. There's always tension simmering just beneath the surface, and it falls to me to keep things from boiling over."

"Like with Gareth?"

Edwin's face hardened. "Gareth had a way of pushing boundaries, of testing my patience. He was... passionate, but his passion often turned into something more confrontational. He didn't approve of the way I managed things. Claimed I was too lenient, that I let people stray from the 'true spirit' of the medieval court."

"So he challenged you?"

Edwin nodded, his jaw tight. "Frequently. He seemed to think that he understood the essence of our group better than anyone else, especially me. But as much as he argued, he would never truly challenge my position. He knew his place in the hierarchy, even if he disliked it."

Elise leaned forward slightly. "And yet, it sounds like he wanted more. Did you ever feel threatened by him?"

Edwin scoffed, a hint of pride flickering in his eyes. "Gareth was ambitious, yes, but he lacked the diplomacy required to lead. He was brash, impatient, and far too inflexible. He could never have managed this group."

Elise made a note, sensing that Edwin's dismissive tone was more defensive than confident. "Did he have allies within the group?"

Edwin frowned, thinking for a moment. "A few, perhaps. His squire, young Elias, admired him. But for the most part, Gareth's abrasive nature isolated him. People respected his skills, but they didn't particularly like him."

"Thank you, Edwin," Elise said, her tone signalling the end of their conversation. Edwin gave her a tight nod, then left the room, his footsteps echoing down the corridor.

Elise glanced at her notes, the puzzle pieces of these relationships beginning to form a picture. There was an undeniable hierarchy within this group, each role carefully constructed, yet prone to rivalry and unrest.

Next to enter was Lady Eleanor. She seemed exhausted, her eyes red from crying, but she offered Elise a warm, albeit strained, smile.

"Thank you for speaking with me, Lady Eleanor," Elise began gently. "Tell me about your role here. I understand you're seen as a... peacekeeper, of sorts."

THE POISONED CHALICE 27

Eleanor nodded, her fingers nervously twisting a ring on her hand. "Yes, I suppose that's true. I've been part of this group for years, and I try to keep things civil, to make sure everyone feels... included. Some of the others can be very... passionate about their roles." She hesitated, glancing down.

"Gareth?" Elise asked.

Eleanor sighed, her expression troubled. "Gareth was... complicated. He had such a strong personality. He could be charming, even captivating, but also... harsh. He didn't tolerate what he saw as weaknesses or frivolities."

"Did you ever witness any direct conflict between Gareth and the others?"

Eleanor's gaze dropped. "Yes. Mostly with Edwin and Isolde. He... criticized them often. Said that they weren't true to the spirit of the reenactment, that they were more concerned with playing lords and ladies than with honouring history."

"Did you agree with him?"

Eleanor's lips pressed into a thin line. "I admired his dedication, but his methods... No, I didn't agree. I thought there was room for both tradition and enjoyment."

Elise studied her for a moment, sensing that Eleanor was holding something back. "Lady Eleanor, did Gareth's behaviour ever go beyond mere criticism?"

Eleanor looked up, her eyes filled with a sadness that seemed older than the evening's events. "I... I think Gareth saw enemies where there were none. He grew bitter over the years, feeling that his love for the past was... misunderstood." She paused, her voice trembling. "He drove people away. In his pursuit of authenticity, he alienated us."

"Thank you," Elise said softly, watching as Eleanor rose and left the room, her shoulders slumped.

Alone again, Elise reviewed her notes. The reenactors' roles were more than just costumes and titles; they were identities woven with ambitions, grudges, and bitter rivalries. Each participant had something to lose and, it seemed, something to hide. It was clear to Elise now that beneath the chivalric vows and courtly titles, there simmered a dark undercurrent—a tension that had finally boiled over, costing Gareth his life.

The pieces were falling into place.

Chapter 6: A Ghostly Grudge

The morning light filtered through the narrow windows of Langford Castle, casting a greyish glow over the stone walls. Elise had barely slept, her mind haunted by fragments of conversations, faces lined with grief, and secrets that lurked beneath polite smiles. She felt the weight of the investigation growing heavier with each interview, as if the castle itself held its breath, waiting for her to uncover what lay hidden within its shadows.

As she made her way through the chilly corridors, a voice stopped her.

"Detective Morrigan."

Elise turned to find Margaret, the elderly woman who had introduced herself as the "keeper of stories" at the reenactment. She stood in the hallway, her posture rigid, her expression tense. There was something urgent in her eyes, a glint that hinted at knowledge beyond what she'd shared the previous day.

"Good morning, Margaret," Elise replied, nodding. "Is there something you'd like to tell me?"

Margaret hesitated, her gaze flickering down the hall before she motioned for Elise to follow her. "Not here. There's too much to say—and too many ears," she murmured, leading Elise down a narrow passage that ended in a small, dimly lit chamber. Once inside, Margaret closed the door behind them and folded her hands, as though preparing herself for something difficult.

"There's something you should know about this place, Detective," she began, her voice barely above a whisper. "Langford Castle has a... history. A dark one. And I fear what happened last night may be connected to it."

Elise raised an eyebrow, intrigued but cautious. "Go on."

Margaret took a deep breath. "Centuries ago, this castle was the site of a bitter feud between two noble families, the Langfords and the Ainsleys. Legend has it that during one of their gatherings—a celebration much like the reenactment feast—an Ainsley lord was poisoned by a member of the Langford family. The weapon was a chalice, a beautiful silver goblet encrusted with rubies, which was said to be cursed after the Ainsley lord's death."

Elise listened carefully, noting the eerie parallels between the legend and Gareth's death. "A cursed chalice," she murmured. "And this chalice... does it still exist?"

Margaret nodded slowly, her gaze distant. "Yes. They say it's kept here in the castle, stored away in a locked chest deep within the archives. Few people know of its existence, but those of us who have been part of the reenactment for years know the story well. The chalice is supposed to bring misfortune to anyone who drinks from it, a legacy of betrayal and revenge passed down through the ages."

"Do you think someone used this chalice to poison Gareth?" Elise asked, her voice laced with scepticism. "Or do you think it's just a story, a legend to add to the castle's mystique?"

Margaret's eyes darkened. "I'm not a superstitious woman, Detective, but I've seen the way people act around that goblet. There are some who believe the curse is real, who think that the spirit of the Ainsley lord still lingers here, seeking revenge for his untimely death. It's possible that someone saw Gareth's ambition as a threat, as something that needed to be stopped."

The idea seemed far-fetched, but Elise couldn't ignore the uncanny resemblance between the tale and Gareth's death. She leaned forward, watching Margaret closely. "Who else knows about this chalice?"

"Most of the long-standing members of the group," Margaret replied. "Edwin, Isolde, Eleanor, and a few others who have been coming to the reenactments for years. They all know the story, even if they don't all believe in it."

Elise's mind raced as she considered the implications. If this cursed chalice truly existed—and if someone had used it in the

THE POISONED CHALICE

reenactment—then Gareth's death wasn't a spur-of-the-moment decision. It was planned, calculated, and possibly even ritualistic.

"Who would have access to the chalice now?" Elise asked, her tone sharp.

Margaret shifted uncomfortably. "It would be locked away in the archives, accessible only to those with the right keys. Edwin has one, as does Lady Isolde. They're the only two who would be able to reach it."

Elise noted this detail, her suspicions about Isolde and Edwin deepening. "Do you think either of them would use the chalice to harm Gareth?"

Margaret hesitated, her gaze dropping. "I don't know, Detective. But I will say this—Gareth was an ambitious man. He pushed people, stepped on toes, and didn't know when to stop. He may have seen himself as noble, but to some, he was a threat."

"Thank you, Margaret," Elise said, her mind already piecing together the information. "You've been very helpful."

As Margaret left the chamber, Elise remained in the dim room, lost in thought. The cursed chalice, an ancient grudge, and a reenactment group filled with ambition and rivalry—it was becoming increasingly clear that Gareth's death was not a simple case of personal vendetta. Someone had used the castle's dark history to send a message, to invoke a legend that would strike fear into the hearts of those involved.

Elise made her way back to the Great Hall, where the reenactors were still gathered, whispering in small groups, their expressions a mix of grief and unease. She spotted Edwin standing near the fireplace, talking in hushed tones with Lady Eleanor, who looked pale and withdrawn. Elise approached them, her footsteps echoing against the stone floor.

"Edwin, Eleanor," she said, her voice calm but commanding. "There's something I need to ask you about the castle's history."

Eleanor looked at her, startled, while Edwin's face remained carefully composed. "Of course, Detective," Edwin replied, his voice even. "What would you like to know?"

"I've heard there's a chalice stored here in the castle archives," Elise began, watching their reactions closely. "One that's tied to an old feud. A cursed chalice."

Eleanor's hand flew to her mouth, her eyes widening. Edwin's expression, however, remained unreadable, his gaze fixed on Elise.

"Yes, I know the story," Edwin said after a pause. "It's an old legend, one we sometimes share with newcomers to add a bit of mystery to the reenactment. But surely you don't think...?"

"I'm considering all possibilities," Elise replied, her gaze unwavering. "This chalice—it was used in the past to poison an Ainsley lord, correct?"

Edwin nodded slowly, as if weighing his words. "That's what the legend says. But it's only a story, Detective. A way to entertain guests and add a sense of history to our gatherings."

Elise noted the flicker of defensiveness in his tone. "Who has access to this chalice?"

Edwin hesitated, glancing at Eleanor, who looked away, her face tense. "Only a few of us," he admitted finally. "Myself, Lady Isolde... and Lady Eleanor. The chest is kept locked, and the keys are... well, they're a privilege given to only a select few."

"Would Gareth have known about it?" Elise asked, shifting her gaze to Eleanor, who seemed visibly uncomfortable.

"Perhaps," Eleanor murmured, her voice barely a whisper. "He was... fascinated by the castle's history. He used to say that our reenactments should honour the darker parts of history, too, that they shouldn't be... sanitized."

Elise's eyes narrowed. "Did he ever speak of using the chalice? Of... invoking this part of Langford's past?"

THE POISONED CHALICE

33

Eleanor shook her head, looking distressed. "No, not directly. But he was drawn to these stories. I often heard him mention that our reenactments should feel real, that we should embrace the truth, however dark it may be."

Elise's gaze returned to Edwin, who stood silently, his face unreadable. "And what about you, Edwin? What's your view on this legend?"

He held her gaze, his expression hardening. "I think it's just that—a legend. We're here to honour history, yes, but not to glorify its violence."

Elise detected a flicker of irritation beneath his words, as if the very question offended him. But she wasn't convinced by his calm demeanour. Gareth's death was a warning, a deliberate echo of the castle's dark history, and someone in this room had intended it to be so.

"Thank you," Elise said finally. "That will be all for now."

As Edwin and Eleanor walked away, Elise felt the weight of the castle's ancient shadows settle around her. The reenactors had brought Langford's history to life, but they had also invited its curses, its grudges, and its ghosts into their midst.

The cursed chalice wasn't just a piece of history. It was a reminder of an ancient feud that had never truly died, a legacy of betrayal woven into the castle's very stones. And as Elise looked around at the solemn faces of the reenactors, she knew that someone here was determined to make sure the past was never forgotten—or forgiven.

Chapter 7: The Knight and His Secrets

Elise sat alone in the antechamber, the thick stone walls and cold draft reminding her of how far from home—and from her usual caseload—she was. Yet as she sifted through her notes on Gareth, she realized that this case had far more layers than she had initially anticipated. Beneath Gareth's knightly persona lay a man with a complicated past, tangled in webs of ambition, grudges, and fierce loyalties.

Elise had requested background information on Gareth Whitmore from her contacts in law enforcement. She now held a stack of files detailing his life, both within the reenactment group and beyond. It didn't take long to see that Gareth had not only made enemies here at Langford Castle but elsewhere in his life, too. His secrets were many, and some were darker than she'd expected.

From her interviews, Elise had already gathered that Gareth was known for his fierce commitment to authenticity. He had elevated himself to a kind of self-styled authority on medieval traditions and combat, insisting that the reenactments should mirror history in all its brutal honesty. For Gareth, this wasn't just a game—it was a way of life, a world in which he could escape the mundane and embody the knightly virtues he revered. But this passion had a cost, and it often put him at odds with others who didn't share his purist view.

Elise began by investigating Gareth's role within the group and his numerous disputes. She spread her notes across the table, listing the names of those he had clashed with most often: Edwin St. Clair, Lady Isolde, and even Lady Eleanor, whose warm disposition masked a subtle disapproval of Gareth's more extreme methods. But it wasn't just within Langford Castle's walls that Gareth had enemies.

A report from his workplace indicated that Gareth had been reprimanded multiple times for "unprofessional conduct" and had been known to get into heated arguments with colleagues. Several complaints painted a picture of a man who was uncompromising, inflexible, and unyielding in his opinions. While his supervisors had tolerated him because of his work ethic, his attitude had soured many relationships, leaving him increasingly isolated.

Elise leaned back, her mind racing through the connections. Gareth's personality, both inside and outside of the reenactment, was rigidly controlled, his values unshakable. But his need for authenticity, his fierce adherence to a code of honour, had created tension and animosity. He demanded the same level of commitment from others that he demanded of himself, often dismissing anyone who didn't live up to his standards.

As she pondered Gareth's motivations, a knock sounded on the door, and Edwin entered, looking tense but resigned to the interrogation that awaited him.

"Detective Morrigan," he greeted, his voice flat. "You asked to speak to me about Gareth's... behaviour?"

"Yes, thank you for coming, Edwin," Elise replied, gesturing for him to sit. "I've been going through my notes, and I'd like your insight into Gareth's role here—and the conflicts he stirred up."

Edwin took a deep breath, running a hand over his neatly combed hair. "Gareth was... intense," he said carefully, his eyes fixed on Elise's. "He believed he was upholding some kind of noble standard. The rest of us, to him, were too casual, too lenient. He'd criticize us for it, even accuse us of 'dishonouring history,' as he put it."

Elise nodded, encouraging him to continue.

"Our disagreements were constant," Edwin went on, his voice tinged with exasperation. "He wanted the reenactments to be brutal, unfiltered, the way he imagined medieval life really was. He couldn't understand that the rest of us came here for enjoyment, for camaraderie. He would look at us with this... contempt, as though we were playing at something sacred to him."

"Did this ever escalate beyond words?" Elise asked, watching his reaction.

Edwin hesitated, and for a moment, Elise saw the shadow of a memory pass over his face. "There was one incident," he said quietly. "Last year, during one of our staged duels. Gareth insisted on using a real blade—nothing lethal, but sharp enough to inflict serious harm if mishandled. I argued against it, but he wouldn't listen. He accused me of being a coward, unworthy of leading the group."

Elise's eyes narrowed. "And what happened?"

"We compromised on a dulled edge," Edwin replied with a sigh. "But he... let's just say he made his displeasure clear. Afterward, he stopped acknowledging my authority altogether. From that point on, Gareth saw himself as the 'true knight' among us and acted accordingly."

"Was there anyone else in the group who supported him?" Elise asked, recalling Isolde's and Eleanor's guarded responses.

Edwin shook his head slowly. "Not really. People respected his skill, sure, but his attitude... it wore on everyone. Even those who admired his dedication kept their distance. They didn't want to get caught in his... crusade."

Elise leaned forward. "What about outside of Langford? Did Gareth bring any trouble from his personal life into the group?"

A flash of something crossed Edwin's face—reluctance, perhaps. But he answered all the same. "He had some... troubles at work. Nothing serious that I know of, but he'd often come here after an argument with a colleague, brimming with anger. I think he saw this place as his refuge, but he brought his conflicts here, too."

"Do you think he felt threatened by anyone here?" Elise pressed.

Edwin hesitated. "If you mean, did he think someone here was out to get him... possibly. Gareth was paranoid. He thought people were trying to undermine him, to make him look weak. In a way, I think he thrived on it."

THE POISONED CHALICE   37

As Edwin finished, Elise sat back, piecing together the image of a man who had built walls around himself, isolating himself within the fortress of his role as a knight. She dismissed Edwin, who left with a strained expression, and called in Elias, Gareth's squire.

The young man shuffled in, visibly shaken. His eyes darted around the room as though expecting Gareth to storm in at any moment, rebuking him for some misstep. Elise gave him a reassuring nod, gesturing for him to sit.

"Thank you for coming, Elias," she said gently. "I know this must be difficult, but I need to understand more about Gareth—both the man and the knight he tried to be."

Elias swallowed, his hands twisting nervously. "Gareth was... he was everything to me. He taught me how to hold a sword, how to stand tall. He... he took me seriously."

"Did he treat you well?" Elise asked, watching his reaction.

Elias hesitated, biting his lip. "He was... strict. He had high standards. He'd get angry if I messed up, but he also... he believed in me. He said I had the makings of a knight."

"But did you ever feel uncomfortable? Did he ever cross a line?" Elise pressed.

The young man's gaze fell to the floor. "Sometimes. He would get so intense, so... angry. He'd talk about honour and duty like they were life and death. I mean, I believed him—I still do. But it scared me, the way he'd talk about it."

"Did Gareth ever mention feeling threatened by anyone here?" she asked.

Elias nodded, looking up with wide eyes. "Yes, he thought Lord Edwin didn't respect him, didn't understand the real knightly code. He said that Edwin wasn't fit to lead, that it was his duty to show everyone what honour really meant." Elias paused, his voice dropping to a whisper. "And he didn't trust Lady Isolde. He said she was always watching him, that she wanted to take him down."

Elise frowned. "Did he say why he felt that way?"

"He thought she wanted to control everything, that she was too focused on... appearances. He thought she didn't care about what was real," Elias whispered. "He said she'd betray anyone to get what she wanted."

A chill ran down Elise's spine as she listened. Gareth's paranoia was evident, but there was a dark intensity to his accusations, a belief that those around him were plotting against him.

"Thank you, Elias," she said softly, standing as he rose to leave. "You've been very helpful."

Alone once more, Elise pondered the evidence before her. Gareth had cultivated enemies both within and outside the reenactment, drawing lines between himself and those who didn't share his ideals. He'd seen betrayal in every corner, convinced himself that his duty was to embody a code no one else believed in as fervently as he did.

But the ghost of an ancient grudge seemed to linger over Langford Castle, tying Gareth's obsessive desire for honour to the castle's cursed chalice and the long-forgotten feud. He had set himself against those who held power, challenged authority, and insisted on following his own path.

And now he was dead, a victim of his own rigid ideals—or of someone who had finally tired of his crusade.

Chapter 8: Lady of Shadows

Elise prepared herself as she waited for Lady Isolde to arrive for her next interview. Of all the figures in the reenactment group, Isolde had intrigued her the most. Poised, intelligent, and fiercely committed to her role, she exuded an air of both authority and mystery. While Gareth had taken on the mantle of chivalry, Isolde embodied the elegance and intrigue of the medieval court, commanding respect and loyalty in equal measure. But as Elise had already gathered, respect and loyalty were not enough to shield one from the darker aspects of ambition and rivalry.

The door opened, and Lady Isolde entered, her dark green gown rustling against the stone floor. Her posture was straight, her expression guarded but calm as she took a seat across from Elise. She met Elise's gaze directly, her eyes steady and unflinching.

"Detective Morrigan," she said, her voice low and smooth. "You wished to speak with me again?"

"Yes, thank you for coming, Lady Isolde," Elise replied, choosing to use Isolde's title as a subtle acknowledgment of the world in which these people were deeply embedded. "I wanted to discuss your relationship with Gareth."

Isolde's expression didn't falter, though a shadow flickered briefly in her eyes. "Gareth and I had a complex relationship, as I'm sure you've gathered."

"Complex how?" Elise pressed, watching her reaction carefully.

Isolde paused, as if weighing her words. "Gareth was... intense," she began. "He was driven by an unwavering belief in his version of knightly honour, which, I think, blinded him to the nuances of what we do here. He saw everything in absolutes—authenticity versus betrayal, loyalty versus dishonour. To him, I was part of the 'problem,' as he put it."

"Why did he see you as a problem?" Elise asked, intrigued.

39

"Because I didn't share his purist approach," Isolde replied, a hint of irritation slipping into her tone. "He believed that our reenactments should be a brutal, exact replication of medieval life, while I... I appreciated the spectacle, the pageantry. I believe there's beauty in history, Detective, and that beauty deserves to be celebrated. But to Gareth, that was sacrilege."

Elise leaned forward slightly. "Did you argue often?"

"More than often," Isolde admitted, a bitter smile tugging at her lips. "But it was more than that. Gareth and I were rivals, yes, but it wasn't always hostile. There was a time when we were close, actually. We both respected each other's commitment and passion. But over the years, that respect eroded. His demands became... unreasonable, and his contempt for my methods grew."

"Did you ever feel threatened by him?" Elise asked, searching her face for any sign of vulnerability.

Isolde hesitated, her eyes dropping to her hands. "Not physically, no. But Gareth had a way of undermining people, of twisting words and situations to make others feel... lesser. He would question my loyalty, my dedication, implying that I was more interested in appearance than authenticity. He used to say that I hid behind a mask of nobility, that I wasn't 'worthy' of the title I'd chosen."

"Did you resent him for that?" Elise pressed, her tone gentle but firm.

Isolde's gaze hardened. "I resented that he couldn't see beyond his own narrow perspective, yes. He refused to understand that people can interpret history differently, that there is no one 'right' way to appreciate the past." She paused, her voice dropping to a near whisper. "But despite all of that... I never wished him harm, Detective. I found his dedication maddening, yes, but it was also part of who he was."

Elise studied Isolde, noting the flicker of frustration and sorrow in her eyes. "Did you see him as an obstacle, though? Someone who stood in the way of your vision for the group?"

THE POISONED CHALICE

Isolde held her gaze, her expression unreadable. "If you mean, did I see him as a rival, then yes. But we were all rivals in some sense, Detective. That's the nature of the court. Ambition, pride, competition—it's woven into the roles we play here. Gareth wasn't the only one with strong opinions."

"Still, Gareth seemed particularly fixated on you," Elise observed. "According to others, he often spoke of you as someone who had betrayed the 'true' spirit of the reenactment."

A faint smile crossed Isolde's face, though there was no warmth in it. "Gareth was paranoid. He saw betrayal in the smallest of actions, perceived enemies where there were none. If I spoke to Edwin, it was because I was 'plotting' against him. If I advocated for less violent reenactments, it was because I was 'weakening' the group. In Gareth's eyes, I was the antithesis of his knightly code."

Elise nodded, letting the silence stretch for a moment before asking, "And what about the chalice?"

Isolde's gaze sharpened, her posture stiffening. "The chalice?" she repeated, a hint of caution in her voice.

"I've heard the story," Elise replied. "An old feud between the Langfords and the Ainsleys, ending with a poisoned chalice—a cursed relic, some would say. You're one of the few who had access to it, Isolde."

Isolde's face remained impassive, but there was a flicker of something—a flash of fear, perhaps—that crossed her eyes. "The chalice is a symbol, Detective, nothing more. It's a piece of history, and we keep it locked away. I would never... it's a relic, yes, but it's also just a story."

Elise raised an eyebrow. "And yet, someone used it last night. Do you know who might have seen that story as more than just a legend?"

Isolde's gaze dropped, her voice lowering. "There are those who believe in the curse, I suppose. Gareth was fascinated by it, obsessed with the notion of fate and betrayal. He would often talk about ancient grudges, about the need for justice in the 'old ways.' I thought he was simply... dramatizing, as he often did. But perhaps he took it more seriously than I realized."

"Did he ever talk about using the chalice?" Elise pressed, sensing an opening.

Isolde hesitated. "Not directly. But he hinted at it, in his own way. He would speak of justice, of punishing those who defied honour. I thought it was all part of his performance, his need to elevate himself as the 'righteous knight.' I didn't think he would actually..."

Her voice trailed off, a shadow crossing her face. Elise noted the sudden vulnerability in her expression, the flicker of guilt. "Is there something you're not telling me, Isolde?"

Isolde took a breath, composing herself. "Gareth and I had a final argument the night before he died. He accused me of undermining him, of conspiring with Edwin to take control of the group. He said... he said that I would regret it."

Elise's eyes narrowed. "Did he threaten you?"

"No, not exactly. It was more of a... warning," Isolde replied, her voice tight. "He believed that I was unfit to lead, that my ideas would destroy everything he'd worked to build. And he made it clear that he would do whatever was necessary to 'protect' the group from me."

"And yet, he's the one who ended up dead," Elise said, her words hanging heavily in the air. "Do you think he knew his life was in danger?"

Isolde's gaze dropped to her hands, her fingers clenching slightly. "I think... Gareth saw enemies where there were none. He was so wrapped up in his role, in his belief that he alone understood the 'true' spirit of the group, that he isolated himself from us. But I never wished him dead, Detective. Rivalries don't have to end in bloodshed."

Elise studied her carefully, noting the flashes of anger, guilt, and something else—a lingering sadness, perhaps. "Did you ever feel guilty for how things ended between you?"

THE POISONED CHALICE 43

A shadow crossed Isolde's face. "Yes," she admitted quietly. "We were once allies, after all. But his bitterness consumed him, and he became... impossible. I resented him, but that resentment didn't drive me to murder."

Elise let her words settle, her own thoughts turning. Isolde's rivalry with Gareth was undeniably fierce, but Elise couldn't shake the feeling that the woman's sorrow was genuine. Still, Isolde's access to the chalice—and her complicated relationship with Gareth—placed her in a precarious position. Whether she had intended to harm him or not, her role in his downfall remained unclear.

"Thank you, Lady Isolde," Elise said finally, signalling the end of the interview. "I may have more questions for you later."

Isolde rose gracefully, giving Elise a nod before leaving the room. As the door closed, Elise sat in silence, piecing together the puzzle of Gareth's life and death. Isolde's rivalry with Gareth ran deep, woven with betrayal, ambition, and a shared history that had twisted into resentment. She'd had motive, means, and opportunity.

But as Elise stared at the closed door, she wondered if Isolde's shadowed role was simply one part of a larger, darker court, one where rivals plotted from behind carefully composed faces and ancient curses awaited those bold enough to wield them.

Chapter 9: The Poisoner's Hand

As dawn broke over Langford Castle, Elise made her way to the forensics tent set up in the courtyard, where the pathologist, Dr. Alan Greene, was waiting with updates. After a night of relentless interviews, Elise was eager for concrete evidence—something that could cut through the maze of rivalries and feuds. If the poison that killed Gareth could be traced, it might finally offer her a direct link to his killer.

Dr. Greene greeted her with a nod, his face set in an expression of grim curiosity. He held a small vial containing the residue from Gareth's goblet. The liquid inside was a murky, dark color, faintly iridescent when it caught the morning light.

"Detective Morrigan," he began, "I think we've uncovered something unusual here."

Elise leaned forward, her gaze fixed on the vial. "What do we have?"

"After conducting preliminary tests, we've determined that the poison used was not a common, modern toxin. It's a blend of several toxic herbs and minerals, most of which were commonly used in medieval Europe," he explained, his tone carefully neutral. "The combination itself is rare—most of these ingredients are difficult to source, and mixing them would require a significant degree of knowledge in historical toxins."

Elise's mind raced. "So we're looking at someone with a deep understanding of medieval poisons—someone who would know how to recreate something like this."

Dr. Greene nodded. "Precisely. This blend contains belladonna, monkshood, and a trace of powdered arsenic. But there's more to it. Whoever mixed this poison did so with remarkable skill. The proportions were precise, and the poison was designed to act quickly, but not immediately, allowing Gareth time to drink and participate in the toast before succumbing."

THE POISONED CHALICE

Elise felt a chill settle over her. This was no accident, no hastily concocted plan. The poisoner had intended for Gareth to die at the height of the feast, a performance as dramatic as any staged scene in their reenactments.

"Could an average person make this?" Elise asked, her voice barely above a whisper.

Dr. Greene shook his head. "No, Detective. This blend would require not only knowledge but access to rare ingredients and, most importantly, the patience to create it. It's not something you'd find in a regular pharmacy or gardening store. The preparation itself is a lengthy, delicate process, with a small margin for error. Whoever did this knew what they were doing."

Elise absorbed this information, her thoughts already turning to the list of suspects. The reenactment group was full of history enthusiasts, each with their own unique skills and knowledge. But this poison pointed to someone with an expertise in herbal lore or medieval alchemy—someone who understood the weight of history and the art of lethal concoctions.

"Thank you, Dr. Greene. This is invaluable," Elise said, her mind whirring. "I have a few suspects who might fit this profile."

Dr. Greene handed her the forensic report, his expression serious. "If you have any specific individuals in mind, I'd suggest looking at those with a strong connection to the castle's history. This blend feels... symbolic. The choice of ingredients isn't just practical; it's meant to send a message."

Elise nodded, her thoughts narrowing to a few likely suspects. Lady Isolde, with her knowledge of the castle's history and dark legends, immediately came to mind. Her rivalry with Gareth was well known, and she had access to the castle's more arcane resources. There was also Edwin St. Clair, who as the leader of the group would likely have some historical knowledge, though he had dismissed Gareth's extreme approach to authenticity. And then there were the fringe members, those who took their roles a bit too seriously, the ones who saw the reenactments as a chance to embody the "real" medieval experience.

Elise left the forensic tent, report in hand, and made her way back toward the castle. She needed to find out who in the group possessed this rare skill set and, perhaps more importantly, who would have had access to the materials required to craft such a poison.

Her first stop was Lady Isolde. Elise found her in one of the castle's smaller chambers, poring over a manuscript illuminated with intricate medieval illustrations. She looked up as Elise entered, her face a mask of practiced calm.

"Detective Morrigan," she greeted, setting the manuscript aside. "To what do I owe this visit?"

Elise took a seat across from her, watching Isolde carefully. "I have some new information about Gareth's death," she said, her tone measured. "The poison used to kill him was a medieval blend. Belladonna, monkshood, and arsenic. It's not something just anyone could make."

Isolde's expression remained neutral, though a flicker of something passed through her eyes—an acknowledgment, perhaps, or a shadow of fear.

"That's fascinating," she replied, folding her hands in her lap. "I suppose it aligns with Gareth's passion for authenticity, doesn't it?"

"It does," Elise replied, her tone unwavering. "And it also aligns with someone who has a deep knowledge of medieval history and herbs—someone like you, Lady Isolde."

Isolde's eyes narrowed slightly, but she didn't falter. "Are you accusing me of poisoning Gareth, Detective?"

"I'm trying to determine who in this group has the skills and resources necessary to create such a blend," Elise replied. "You have a reputation for knowing the castle's history, for being interested in the... darker aspects of our past. You even had access to the chalice, which we now know has ties to this very type of poisoning."

THE POISONED CHALICE

47

Isolde exhaled, a hint of irritation flashing across her face. "Yes, Detective, I know the history. And yes, I appreciate the darker parts of it. But knowledge and appreciation do not make me a killer."

"Then help me understand," Elise pressed. "Who else here would have the knowledge to recreate a medieval poison? Who else would even know where to start?"

Isolde tilted her head, considering the question. "If I'm honest, there aren't many. But if you're looking for knowledge of herbs, you might speak with Lady Eleanor. She has an extensive background in botany and often creates herbal remedies as part of her role here. She's quite gifted in that area."

Elise noted this, her mind turning to Lady Eleanor, whose quiet demeanour and gentle nature had made her seem an unlikely suspect. Yet, if she possessed the knowledge of herbs necessary to craft such a poison, she, too, couldn't be overlooked.

"Thank you, Lady Isolde," Elise said, standing. "This has been... enlightening."

Isolde gave a slight nod, watching her with a sharp, assessing gaze. "If I were you, Detective, I would remember that in the court, nothing is as it seems. People wear their masks here well."

Elise left the chamber, her thoughts churning. Isolde's words echoed in her mind. Nothing is as it seems. She knew this already, of course, but it served as a reminder of the complexity of this case. The reenactors wore layers upon layers of roles, both real and imagined, and each one added another barrier between her and the truth.

Elise found Lady Eleanor in the castle's herb garden, nestled within a walled courtyard. The older woman looked up as Elise approached, a soft smile on her face.

"Detective Morrigan," Eleanor greeted warmly, setting aside a basket filled with sprigs of lavender and rosemary. "How can I help you?"

Elise studied her carefully. "I need to ask you some questions about... medieval herbs. Specifically, your knowledge of toxic plants."

Eleanor's face paled slightly, but she didn't falter. "I... I have some knowledge, yes. It's part of the persona I've built here. I play the castle's healer, someone who would understand both remedies and... poisons."

"Does that knowledge include creating a poison like the one used on Gareth?" Elise asked, her gaze steady.

Eleanor's hands trembled slightly as she folded them together. "I know how such a blend could be made, yes. But I would never... I would never do such a thing, Detective. I cared for Gareth, despite his flaws. He was part of our community."

"Do you know if anyone else has this knowledge?" Elise pressed.

Eleanor hesitated. "There are a few who might, but none with as much experience as myself. And yet... I would have noticed if anyone had taken ingredients from the garden. Monkshood, belladonna—they aren't common herbs, and they're kept in a separate section for safety."

Elise nodded, considering Eleanor's words. "Could anyone have taken those herbs without you knowing?"

Eleanor shook her head. "I doubt it. I tend to them carefully. But if someone were determined... perhaps."

Elise thanked Eleanor and left, her mind awash with possibilities. Both Isolde and Eleanor possessed the knowledge necessary to recreate the poison, though their motivations differed. Was it Lady Isolde, Gareth's rival, who resented his purist vision? Or was it Lady Eleanor, hiding a secret she hadn't yet revealed?

As Elise returned to the castle, the weight of the investigation pressed down on her. The poison had revealed the hand of a master, someone with both the knowledge and the ruthlessness to plan Gareth's death with chilling precision.

She now knew two things for certain: Gareth's murder was a carefully crafted act, and someone within the court had taken history's darker secrets and brought them into the present.

Chapter 10: A Message from Beyond

Elise was combing through Gareth's personal belongings, stored temporarily in a small, dimly lit room within the castle, when she found it. Tucked between the pages of a leather-bound journal, a piece of folded parchment had caught her eye. The parchment was old and yellowed, with a faint musty smell, its edges frayed. The ink, however, was fresh, as if it had been written in recent weeks.

She unfolded it carefully, her heart beating a little faster as she read the words scrawled in Gareth's bold, uneven handwriting:

"They watch me from the shadows, circling like wolves. Trust none of them, for they are cloaked in smiles and false loyalties. Honor is a mask they wear to conceal their true intentions. They would see me fall, to remove the thorn that I have become. I am certain now: one among them plots my end. I must be vigilant, lest they strike without warning."

The words felt like an echo from another time, as if Gareth had penned them in the throes of paranoia and fear, alone with his thoughts in the dead of night. Elise read the note again, each line sparking new questions. Gareth had believed someone intended to kill him, and he'd gone to the lengths of writing it down—perhaps as a final testament, or as a way to keep his own fear in check.

Setting the note aside, Elise delved deeper into Gareth's journal. Most of it was a strange mixture of personal musings and meticulous notes on medieval combat and chivalry. There were sketches of armour designs, notes on battle tactics, and even excerpts from medieval texts that Gareth had copied down, his reverence for knightly ideals evident in every line. But scattered among these entries were references to the very real feuds that had grown within the reenactment group, hints of his escalating distrust of certain members.

One entry, dated just a week before his death, caught her attention:

"Isolde has become a serpent in my midst, charming the court while twisting its values. She would see herself crowned if she could, dethroning all that is sacred here. I know her game, and I will not yield to her empty pageantry. Edwin is blind to it, as always, more concerned with his title than the truth. And Eleanor—how she simpers and soothes! But beneath her kindness lies another's ambition."

Elise felt a shiver run through her as she read his words. Gareth's paranoia seemed to have spread to every corner of the group, infecting his view of each member. His suspicions were vivid and damning, as though he'd convinced himself that no one around him was trustworthy. He saw Isolde as a usurper, Edwin as a weak leader, and Eleanor as a deceptively gentle manipulator.

The note and journal entries were more than a glimpse into Gareth's mind—they were a roadmap of his fears, each entry another layer of distrust, another crack in the foundation of their fragile community. He had grown to see himself as the last true knight, surrounded by people who either opposed him or failed to meet his standards.

Elise's thoughts were interrupted by a soft knock on the door. She looked up to see Elias standing in the doorway, his eyes downcast and his hands nervously clasped in front of him.

"Detective Morrigan," he said quietly, stepping inside. "I... I heard you were looking through Gareth's things. I thought you might need help with... with understanding him."

Elise gestured for him to come in, grateful for the perspective he might provide. "Thank you, Elias. I found a note in Gareth's belongings—a note suggesting he feared someone in the group was planning to kill him."

Elias's face went pale, and he swallowed hard. "He... he often spoke like that, Detective. Gareth believed he was surrounded by people who didn't understand him, people who wanted him gone."

"Did he ever tell you why he felt this way?" Elise asked, watching him closely.

THE POISONED CHALICE

Elias hesitated, his gaze drifting to the floor. "He said they wanted to silence him, that they were afraid of his... his commitment. He thought that Isolde saw him as an obstacle, that she wanted to run the group her own way, without anyone questioning her. And Edwin... he thought Edwin was weak, that he wouldn't stand up for the traditions Gareth valued."

Elise nodded, taking in Elias's words. "And what about Eleanor?"

A flicker of uncertainty crossed Elias's face. "He respected her, I think, but he didn't trust her. He thought she was too... too accommodating. He said she was always smiling, always making peace, but that it was just a way to keep people close without really standing for anything."

"Did he ever mention receiving threats or seeing anyone act suspiciously toward him?" Elise pressed.

Elias shook his head. "Not directly, no. But he was convinced that they were plotting behind his back. He told me to watch everyone carefully, that they were all 'two-faced courtiers.'"

Elise sighed, sensing that Gareth's paranoia had likely pushed people further away, deepening his isolation. "Did Gareth ever keep a list or make a plan of any kind? Was he documenting his suspicions, perhaps?"

Elias bit his lip, seeming torn. "He didn't write it down, but... he started giving me instructions. He'd tell me who to keep an eye on, when to report back to him about certain conversations. He was so sure that someone would eventually turn on him. He thought he was the last defence against... betrayal."

Elise regarded Elias with a mixture of sympathy and unease. Gareth's delusions had drawn this young squire into his spiral of fear and suspicion, convincing him to play the role of an informer. She could see the guilt etched on Elias's face, the weight of secrets he hadn't been prepared to carry.

"Elisa," she said gently, "do you think he was right? Do you think someone actually intended to harm him?"

Elias looked away, his voice barely a whisper. "I don't know, Detective. I believed him... but after what happened, I don't know what to believe anymore. Maybe he was just... seeing enemies where there were none. But then again... he's dead now, isn't he?"

The stark truth of his words hung heavy in the air. Gareth had indeed died, and while his paranoia might have been exaggerated, it had not been unfounded. Someone had acted on his suspicions—whether to silence him, remove him as a threat, or fulfil a twisted notion of justice.

After dismissing Elias, Elise sat alone with Gareth's note and journal, feeling the weight of their contents settle over her. The words read like a final, unspoken cry for help, written by a man who'd been unable to trust even those closest to him.

She turned her attention back to the note, studying Gareth's choice of words. "They watch me from the shadows... cloaked in smiles and false loyalties." It was as if Gareth had believed his life had become a medieval drama, with everyone playing a part in his inevitable downfall.

And yet, there was one phrase that stood out to Elise more than the rest: "One among them plots my end."

Whoever had poisoned Gareth had been meticulous, careful, knowledgeable. It wasn't a crime of passion but a carefully orchestrated act, one that could have taken days or even weeks of planning. Whoever was responsible had fed off of Gareth's own paranoia, using it as cover for their own dark intentions.

Elise closed the journal, her resolve hardening. She would take Gareth's cryptic warnings seriously, even if they seemed driven by fear. Somewhere in his tangled web of rivalries, in his suspicion and doubt, the truth waited to be uncovered.

THE POISONED CHALICE

With this new insight into Gareth's state of mind, Elise knew she had to reevaluate everyone's motives. Gareth may have been paranoid, but he wasn't necessarily wrong. If one among them had indeed plotted his end, then she would have to look beyond the roles and masks, uncovering what lay beneath the false loyalties and hidden grudges of Langford's court.

And, Elise realized, she would have to act quickly. The poisoner had already struck once.

Chapter 11: The Squire's Burden

Elise found Elias sitting alone in the castle's outer courtyard, his shoulders hunched, eyes distant. He looked even younger than his years, a slight figure clad in the simple tunic of a squire, his face lined with worry and exhaustion. She approached him slowly, noting the way he barely reacted to her presence—a young man worn down by guilt, secrets, and fear.

"Elias," Elise said gently, taking a seat beside him on the stone bench. "I wanted to talk to you again about Sir Gareth."

Elias looked up, startled, as if he hadn't expected anyone to join him. His eyes darted around nervously before he nodded, his voice a strained whisper. "Yes, Detective?"

"There's something I need you to be honest with me about," she began, her tone firm but kind. "Gareth left behind a note, suggesting he believed someone was after him. I need to know if you saw anything unusual in the days leading up to his death—anything that might confirm his suspicions."

Elias swallowed hard, his hands wringing together as he avoided her gaze. "I... I didn't know he'd written something like that," he admitted, his voice shaky. "But... but he did seem more on edge than usual. He told me to be careful, to keep an eye out for anyone who might try to... get close to him."

"Did anything stand out to you?" Elise pressed, leaning in. "Even something that seemed small or unimportant?"

Elias's gaze dropped to his hands, his fingers tightening. He hesitated, as if weighing whether to speak, and Elise sensed that this reluctance wasn't merely nervousness. Whatever he was hiding, it was something that deeply unsettled him.

"I... I did see something," he said finally, his voice barely above a whisper. "The night before he... before the feast, I went to find him.

THE POISONED CHALICE

He'd left something in his quarters, and I was bringing it to him. When I found him, he was outside, near the north tower."

Elise's attention sharpened. "And?"

Elias shifted uncomfortably. "He wasn't alone. There was someone else with him—a figure cloaked in black. They were standing close, speaking in low voices. It was dark, so I couldn't see the other person's face, but... they seemed tense. Like they were arguing."

"What were they arguing about?" Elise asked, her voice calm but insistent.

Elias shook his head. "I couldn't hear everything, but I caught bits and pieces. Gareth was accusing them of... betrayal. He kept saying things like, 'You think I don't know what you're planning?' and, 'I won't let you ruin what we've built here.' He was angry, more angry than I'd ever seen him."

"And the other person?" Elise prompted. "Did they respond?"

Elias's face paled, and he looked down, his fingers twisting anxiously. "They were trying to calm him down, I think. I heard them say something like, 'You're being paranoid, Gareth,' and, 'This is all in your head.' But Gareth wouldn't listen. He told them that they were making a grave mistake, that he knew everything."

Elise leaned forward, her voice low. "Did you recognize this person? Even a hint of who it might be?"

Elias hesitated, his eyes flicking to her for a moment before he shook his head. "I... I'm not sure, Detective. I couldn't see their face, and their voice was muffled. But... but the way they spoke... it felt familiar. Like it was someone from our group."

Elise considered this, her mind racing through the list of suspects. A clandestine meeting the night before Gareth's death, an argument steeped in accusations of betrayal—it painted a picture of someone deeply involved in the reenactment, someone who'd had a personal stake in Gareth's fate. The figures who came to mind were Edwin,

Isolde, and Eleanor, each of whom had complex histories and motives where Gareth was concerned.

"Elias, did Gareth tell you anything else about his suspicions?" Elise asked, choosing her words carefully. "Did he ever mention someone specific?"

Elias hesitated, biting his lip. "He didn't name names, but... he kept telling me to watch Lady Isolde. He was convinced that she was plotting against him, that she wanted to... take control of the group. He thought she was trying to undermine everything he stood for."

Elise nodded, absorbing this information. Isolde had been one of Gareth's primary rivals, her approach to the reenactment at odds with his rigid vision. Their clashes had been well-known, and Gareth's paranoia had turned her from a mere rival into a potential enemy in his eyes.

But Elise knew that Isolde wasn't the only one Gareth had distrusted. The note she'd found and the journal entries painted a picture of a man surrounded by perceived threats, each figure cast in the role of betrayer or usurper.

"Thank you for telling me this, Elias," she said softly. "I know this must be difficult for you."

Elias looked up at her, his face a mixture of relief and fear. "I just... I wish I'd done something. I wish I'd told someone what I saw. Maybe... maybe he wouldn't have..."

His voice trailed off, a tremor in his words. Elise reached out, placing a reassuring hand on his shoulder. "You did what you could, Elias. Sometimes, people's fears lead them to push others away. Gareth's suspicions were his own burden, one that he chose to carry alone."

Elias nodded, his gaze dropping again. "I just hope... I hope you find out who did this. He didn't deserve to die like that, Detective. He was... he was flawed, yes, but he cared. Even if he didn't always show it, he believed in honour."

THE POISONED CHALICE 57

Elise rose, her mind focused and her purpose clear. Elias's story had added a new layer to the mystery, an encounter that hinted at a deeper scheme hidden beneath the surface. The unknown figure, cloaked in secrecy, had met Gareth under the cover of darkness, only hours before his death. It was no coincidence.

As she left Elias in the courtyard, Elise turned her thoughts to Isolde, Edwin, and Eleanor. One of them, or someone close to them, had confronted Gareth that night, stoking his paranoia, perhaps even provoking him further. She would need to revisit each of them, probing their actions and alibis more thoroughly, but first she would examine the north tower.

Reaching the tower's entrance, she surveyed the area. The stones were weathered, dark with age, and the heavy iron gate stood slightly ajar, allowing her to step inside. The interior was dimly lit, dust motes swirling in the thin shafts of light filtering through the narrow windows.

She scanned the ground, noting scuff marks in the dust near the walls. As she traced the faint marks, she realized they led to a narrow alcove. Something glinted faintly in the shadows—a small, ornate button, likely from a cloak or jacket, its silver surface decorated with a delicate knot pattern.

Elise held the button up, examining it carefully. She hadn't seen anyone wearing a cloak adorned with this type of button so far, but it was a distinct style, unique enough that it might lead her to the owner. She slipped it into her pocket, determined to identify its source.

Leaving the tower, she returned to the castle, her mind racing. The evidence was piling up, each clue forming part of a larger, darker picture. A confrontation between Gareth and an unknown figure, a button left behind in a moment of tension, and Gareth's own words pointing to betrayal—each piece was a thread in the web that surrounded his death.

As she walked back through the castle corridors, she felt a renewed sense of purpose. Gareth's paranoia may have clouded his view of his companions, but there was truth hidden within his fears. Someone had used his suspicions, played on his insecurities, and orchestrated his end with chilling precision.

And now Elise had something to go on—a glimpse of the poisoner's hand, and a piece of evidence that might just unmask them.

The court was drawing closer to revelation, its shadows thinning in the light of truth.

Chapter 12: The Hidden Chamber

Elise had spent the better part of the morning reviewing the castle's blueprints and historical records, hoping to find any architectural oddities that could hide a secret. Langford Castle was steeped in centuries of mystery, and she'd already noted a few mentions of "hidden alcoves" and "undiscovered rooms" in old documents. However, most of these accounts had been dismissed as legends or mere ghost stories, the kinds of tales designed to fascinate visitors and attract thrill-seekers. But something about Gareth's death and the strange mix of betrayal and secrets within this reenactment group made Elise take these stories more seriously.

Her intuition paid off when she found a reference in a dusty journal kept by a previous owner of the castle. In a faded, barely legible scrawl, the journal spoke of a "room of shadows," concealed behind an old tapestry in the west wing. The castle's owners had reportedly used the room during times of strife, a private place to hold meetings and even trials.

Elise made her way to the west wing, passing by servants who moved about their tasks, unaware of the hidden history woven into the stone walls. She reached a dimly lit hallway where an ancient tapestry hung, its edges frayed and its colors muted. The tapestry depicted a scene of knights in armour, banners held high, with one figure seemingly watching the others with an intensity that sent a chill down Elise's spine. She ran her fingers along the edge of the tapestry, feeling for any hidden latch or indentation.

And then—there. Her fingers brushed against a small lever concealed behind the fabric. Taking a deep breath, Elise pulled it, and a soft click echoed in the silence. A narrow section of the wall swung open, revealing a steep, spiral staircase descending into the darkness.

Elise took out her flashlight, its beam slicing through the musty air as she began her descent. The stairs were cramped and uneven, their stones worn by time. She moved carefully, each step echoing faintly in the confined space. Finally, she reached the bottom, where a heavy wooden door, bound in iron, waited for her.

Pushing the door open, Elise stepped into a hidden chamber. The room was small but filled with relics of the past, each item seemingly frozen in time. Ancient weapons hung from the walls, their metal dull but well-preserved. A suit of armour, heavily adorned and taller than most, stood in one corner, its hollow eyes staring into the dim room. Shelves lined with artifacts filled one side of the room: daggers, parchments, and jars containing unknown substances that had likely once been used in ancient rituals.

The center of the room, however, was what truly caught her attention.

A large, circular table stood in the middle, covered with symbols carved into the wood—intricate patterns, knots, and dark shapes that Elise recognized from her own research as medieval symbols for loyalty, betrayal, and justice. Each symbol seemed to represent an aspect of the feudal code, but woven together, they formed something darker, as if the table had once been used as a place for judging, condemning, or even plotting.

On the far side of the table, Elise saw something that made her heart race. A tarnished silver chalice, its surface inlaid with rubies and faintly inscribed with words in Latin: "Fides et Perfidia"—Faith and Betrayal. It matched the description of the cursed chalice she'd heard about, the very object connected to the dark legend of Langford Castle.

Moving closer, Elise examined the chalice, feeling a chill as she noted a faint discoloration inside, as if some liquid had once stained the metal. The sight of it sent a shiver down her spine. If this was the chalice used in Gareth's poisoning, then the murder was no mere act of revenge—it was part of something larger, a twisted reenactment of Langford's darkest history.

THE POISONED CHALICE 61

Elise's gaze fell on an open book lying beside the chalice. Its pages were filled with old script, detailing various punishments and methods of ensuring "justice" in feudal times. Several entries had been underlined, most notably passages about the use of poison in trials, an ancient method for determining innocence or guilt by survival.

She scanned the pages, each line more disturbing than the last. Whoever had come here before her had studied these methods, perhaps even drawn inspiration from them. This wasn't just a murder—it was a ritual, meticulously designed to echo the brutal history of Langford Castle. Gareth's death had been intended as a statement, a message to all those in the group.

As she continued searching, Elise found another clue that deepened the mystery. Tucked under the chalice was a piece of parchment, bearing a symbol she recognized from the carvings on the table—a knot with a dagger piercing through it, the medieval symbol for treachery. And underneath the symbol were words written in a strong, looping hand:

"The sins of the past demand justice, for blood is owed to those who betray the ancient code. Let it be known, the court remembers."

Elise's pulse quickened. The note was cryptic, but its message was clear: someone in the group believed they were carrying out justice for a perceived betrayal, reenacting the ancient feuds of the castle. The chalice, the poison, the symbols—all of it was part of a twisted notion of medieval justice, a ritual punishment for those deemed unworthy.

She carefully folded the note and placed it in her pocket, then turned her attention to the shelves. Among the dusty tomes and scrolls, one book in particular caught her eye. Bound in cracked leather, it bore no title, only a single word carved into the spine: Coniuratio—Latin for "Conspiracy." She flipped through its pages, finding lists of names, descriptions of alliances, and even hand-drawn maps of the castle, indicating hidden passageways and rooms. The book was a guide to Langford's secrets, a map for those who sought power within its walls.

The most unsettling discovery was a list written near the back, detailing "roles" and "titles" for various individuals within the reenactment group. Beside some names were notes: loyal, traitor, deceiver, each designation a damning label that hinted at deep-seated divisions and alliances within the group. And beside Gareth's name, in dark, bold letters, was a single word: judged.

Elise's mind raced as she pieced together the implications. Someone within the group had assumed the role of a judge, casting Gareth as the guilty party. This wasn't merely a reenactment—it was a medieval court brought to life, and Gareth's death was the sentence.

She scanned the rest of the book, finding notes on rituals, oaths, and symbols that connected to each member of the group in some way. The titles, the hidden accusations, the concept of "judging" based on ancient codes—it was as if someone had taken it upon themselves to become the arbiter of Langford's legacy, determining who was worthy and who was a threat to the "honour" of their fictional court.

As she turned to leave the hidden chamber, Elise felt the weight of her discovery settle on her shoulders. She knew she was on the brink of uncovering something that went beyond murder—a system of twisted loyalty and retribution that had become a deadly reality for the members of this group.

Returning to the main part of the castle, she resolved to confront each of the reenactors with the evidence she'd found, beginning with Edwin and Isolde, the two figures most deeply entangled in the group's hierarchy. The chalice, the symbols, and the concept of betrayal were woven into the fabric of this court, each thread leading back to someone who believed themselves righteous enough to punish others.

Elise would not leave Langford until the person responsible had been brought to light. This hidden chamber, with its dark relics and symbols, had unveiled a conspiracy older than any reenactment, a conspiracy that had claimed a life under the guise of "justice."

THE POISONED CHALICE

And she was determined to reveal the true face behind the mask of this twisted court.

Chapter 13: Blood Ties

Elise sat in the castle library, a thick binder of genealogical records spread open on the table in front of her. The air smelled of old parchment and ink, and the dim lighting cast a warm glow over the yellowed pages. She had spent hours combing through the records, tracing the lineages of Langford Castle's original owners, their rival families, and the inheritance disputes that had simmered for generations. With each new page, Elise felt as though she was peeling back layers of a centuries-old wound, one that had been passed down, unresolved, through the bloodlines of those who now stood in the shadows of the castle's walls.

The records revealed a complex web of connections between the current reenactors and the families that had once laid claim to Langford Castle. Many of them were descendants of families with a direct stake in the castle's history, people whose ancestors had fought, betrayed, and even killed for a place within its storied walls.

It wasn't just about reenactment for some of these people—it was personal. Elise could now see how ancient loyalties, rivalries, and ambitions might still simmer beneath their roles.

Her first revelation involved Edwin St. Clair. Edwin's family, she discovered, had deep ties to Langford Castle. The St. Clair line could be traced back to a barony that had once controlled a large portion of the surrounding lands, a barony that had been stripped from them during a feud with the Langford family. According to the records, the St. Clairs had attempted to reclaim their lands multiple times, each attempt thwarted by the Langfords, who had solidified their claim through marriage and political manoeuvring.

Edwin's ancestors had been stripped of titles and influence, and the bitterness of that loss had lingered. It was clear that for Edwin, Langford Castle represented not just a role to play, but a legacy to restore, a piece of family history he could never fully reclaim. Perhaps

THE POISONED CHALICE

this explained his drive to preside over the reenactment as "lord" of the court. It was a way of assuming, if only in play, the role his family had once held in reality.

The second connection Elise found was even more intriguing. Lady Isolde—real name Clara Whitford—was a descendant of the Ainsley family, the same family mentioned in the legend of the cursed chalice. The Ainsleys had once been allies of the Langfords, but a betrayal over a marriage alliance had caused a vicious feud that ended in bloodshed. According to the records, the Ainsley family believed they'd been cheated out of their rightful claim to Langford Castle and had carried a grudge against the Langfords for generations. The poisoned chalice that had supposedly killed the Ainsley lord centuries ago was rumoured to be the cursed symbol of that betrayal.

For Clara, the reenactment was likely a complex stage for honouring her heritage while reviving old enmities. Her character as "Lady Isolde" was powerful, poised, and cunning—traits that mirrored those of her Ainsley ancestors. Her rivalry with Gareth, who had wanted to embody the very essence of chivalric honour, might have felt to her like history repeating itself.

As Elise connected the dots, another name came to light: Lady Eleanor, known for her warmth and kindness. Eleanor's family, the Montforts, had been mediators in the original feud between the Langfords and the Ainsleys. They had played both sides, acting as trusted allies to each family, even as they carefully positioned themselves to benefit regardless of who emerged victorious. This history of diplomacy and double-dealing had persisted, passed down as a family tradition of subtle influence and hidden power.

Eleanor's role in the reenactment as the "heart" of the court took on a new significance now. Her kindness could be a reflection of her family's historical approach—smiling, supporting, and diffusing tension while ensuring they remained central to the balance of power. Eleanor's peacekeeping demeanour wasn't just an act of good will; it was a performance honed over generations of family strategy. In the world of Langford Castle's court, Eleanor was the glue that held the feuding groups together, but it was a role that might require careful, quiet manipulation.

Elise sat back, absorbing these revelations. The reenactment group was not simply a gathering of history enthusiasts. These people were living out family legacies, some of them stepping into roles that had haunted their bloodlines for centuries. To some, this event was an opportunity to rewrite history, to take on the title or the power that had once been denied to their ancestors. For others, it was a reminder of the grudges and betrayals that had carved their families' fates.

It was no wonder tensions had run high among them. Gareth, with his fierce commitment to "true" medieval honour, had likely disrupted this delicate balance. His insistence on rigid authenticity and his disdain for compromise had made him a polarizing figure. To Edwin, Gareth's extreme vision might have felt like an insult to the St. Clair legacy, a challenge to the authority he believed was rightfully his. For Isolde, Gareth's commitment to knightly ideals could have felt like a personal attack, a reminder of the Ainsley betrayal and their claim to Langford.

And for Eleanor, Gareth's disruptive presence had likely threatened the harmony she worked so carefully to maintain.

Elise's mind buzzed with these connections as she closed the binder and rose from her seat. She knew she needed to speak to each of these key players, confronting them not just about their roles, but about their family histories and how these histories intersected with the reenactment.

She began with Edwin, whom she found in the Great Hall, adjusting a tapestry. She approached him quietly, and he turned, surprised.

"Detective Morrigan," he greeted, a touch wary. "Is there something I can help you with?"

THE POISONED CHALICE

"Yes, Edwin, there is," Elise replied, her tone steady. "I've been looking into Langford Castle's history and your family's connection to it. You're a St. Clair, aren't you?"

A flash of something crossed his face—pride, perhaps, tinged with resentment. "Yes, I am. The St. Clairs were once noblemen here, lords of this land until... well, until history took its course."

"Would you say that your role here is, in part, a way of reclaiming that lost legacy?" Elise asked, watching him closely.

Edwin straightened, his eyes sharpening. "I suppose you could say that. My family lost what was rightfully theirs. Langford was taken from us, passed down through marriages and power grabs. This reenactment gives me a way to... honour that past, even if it's only in spirit."

Elise nodded thoughtfully. "And how did you feel about Gareth's approach? Did it ever feel like a challenge to your own vision?"

Edwin's expression darkened. "Gareth was... difficult. He saw everything in black and white, as if chivalry and honour were absolutes. He didn't understand the history of this place, what it means to my family. To him, Langford was a backdrop for his ideals, not the resting place of centuries of legacy."

Leaving Edwin with a polite nod, Elise next sought out Lady Isolde, finding her in the gardens, her posture elegant, gaze fixed on the distant hills. She turned as Elise approached, her face a mask of calm.

"Detective Morrigan," she greeted smoothly. "To what do I owe the pleasure?"

"I wanted to speak to you about your family, the Ainsleys," Elise said, watching her carefully. "Your ancestors were once allies of the Langfords, weren't they?"

Isolde's lips curved into a faint smile, though her eyes remained wary. "Yes, that's correct. The Ainsleys and Langfords were once bound by marriage alliances and shared interests. But as with all power, alliances are... fragile."

"And this chalice," Elise continued, "the one tied to your family's curse. Do you feel connected to that story?"

Isolde's gaze turned distant, her voice soft. "It's hard not to, Detective. The chalice represents betrayal, a reminder that loyalty is often an illusion. When Gareth insisted on absolute honour, he failed to see that power is rarely so pure."

Elise left Isolde deep in thought and sought out Eleanor, who was arranging flowers in the main corridor, her gentle hands working with care.

"Lady Eleanor," Elise greeted, watching as she looked up, smiling warmly.

"Detective," Eleanor replied, her expression open and kind. "How can I help you?"

"Your family, the Montforts, they acted as mediators in the old feud between the Langfords and the Ainsleys, didn't they?" Elise asked, noting Eleanor's brief pause.

"Yes," she admitted. "The Montforts were always... adaptable. We saw ourselves as neutral ground, a family that believed in peace, even if it meant staying close to both sides."

"Do you see yourself in that role here?" Elise asked.

Eleanor smiled softly, a touch of sadness in her eyes. "Yes. I try to keep the peace, Detective, though it isn't always easy. Sometimes, one side must be... reminded of what's best for everyone."

Elise felt a chill, recognizing the weight of Eleanor's words. As she walked away, she realized that Langford Castle wasn't just haunted by its history. It was haunted by those who still lived within it, those whose blood ties and ancient feuds pulsed just beneath the surface.

Gareth's death wasn't a random act. It was rooted in these legacies, these grudges reborn, and Elise knew that if she was to solve this mystery, she would have to dig even deeper into the castle's twisted past.

Chapter 14: A Poisoned Past

Elise sat across from the castle's resident historian, Dr. Ambrose Hale, a man well into his eighties with a sharp mind and a lifetime of knowledge about Langford Castle's dark history. His hair was a wild nest of white, and his eyes held the glint of someone who had spent a lifetime uncovering secrets. When she'd asked him about the legends of Langford, he'd given her a knowing smile and invited her into his private study, a cluttered room lined with shelves of ancient books, parchments, and artifacts.

"So," Dr. Hale began, settling into a creaky leather chair, "you're here to learn about the legend of the poisoned chalice. A tale as old as the stones of Langford itself."

Elise nodded, leaning forward, eager for any information that might cast light on Gareth's murder. "I understand that the chalice is connected to an ancient feud between noble families. I'd like to know the full story, if you're willing to share it."

Dr. Hale chuckled softly, his eyes narrowing with a mix of amusement and gravitas. "Ah, Langford's cursed chalice... The story has been passed down through the generations, though details have shifted as they do with time. But some things remain the same: betrayal, revenge, and, of course, poison."

He gestured toward a dusty tome on his desk, a thick, leather-bound book adorned with gold embossing, the spine marked with the word Historiae Langfordi. With careful hands, he opened it to a page marked with a yellowing ribbon, revealing an intricate illustration of a nobleman slumped over a grand banquet table, a jewelled chalice overturned beside him, dark liquid dripping onto the tablecloth.

"This," he said, his voice dropping to a near-whisper, "is the story of Lord Ambrose Langford, a proud and ruthless man who ruled over Langford Castle with an iron fist. Ambrose's family had secured their control over the land through cunning alliances and, occasionally, force. But in his later years, he grew paranoid, convinced that others coveted his wealth and power."

Elise listened intently as Dr. Hale continued, his voice rich with a storyteller's cadence. "To maintain his hold on Langford, Ambrose arranged a marriage between his only daughter, Eleanor Langford, and a member of the Ainsley family, then a rising power in the region. The marriage was supposed to solidify an alliance and keep his enemies close. But Eleanor despised her new husband, Lord Robert Ainsley. He was cruel, arrogant, and cared more for his own ambitions than the promises he'd made."

"Elise nodded, intrigued by the parallels with the modern-day reenactors' family ties. "And did this marriage go as planned?"

Dr. Hale shook his head, a knowing smile on his face. "Far from it. Lady Eleanor was not the type to be used as a pawn, and she found a lover—someone she trusted, someone who despised her husband as much as she did. And when Robert discovered this betrayal, he confronted her, threatening her with ruin and demanding she cut off her lover."

"But she didn't?" Elise asked, already guessing the answer.

Dr. Hale's eyes sparkled. "No. Instead, during a grand banquet held to mark the union of the two families, Eleanor's lover—a knight loyal to her family—slipped a lethal blend of poisons into Lord Robert's chalice. According to legend, the mixture was an ancient concoction used in trials of treachery, a deadly mix that would cause a slow but certain death."

Elise's mind raced as she absorbed the story. "So Lord Robert was poisoned at his own wedding feast?"

"Indeed," Dr. Hale replied, his voice reverent. "As the story goes, Lord Robert drank from the chalice, raising a toast to his new family. Moments later, he collapsed, clutching his throat as the life drained from him. Chaos erupted, but Lady Eleanor remained calm. She

THE POISONED CHALICE

watched as he died, knowing she'd taken back control of her life, even if it meant violating every code of loyalty her family held."

"And what happened to her?" Elise asked, captivated.

"She was spared," Dr. Hale said, his voice tinged with dark amusement. "Her father, Lord Ambrose, protected her, claiming the poisoning was an act of fate, punishment for Ainsley's cruelty. But others believed she had unleashed a curse upon the castle by poisoning her husband. Ever since that night, the chalice has been said to hold a dark power, a curse for any who would attempt to play with loyalty and betrayal in Langford."

Elise glanced down at the illustration of the poisoned lord, her mind reeling with the implications. The curse of the chalice wasn't just a legend—it was a symbol of vengeance, revenge against perceived betrayals. She could see how this story, handed down through generations, might have fuelled the motives of those now connected to Langford Castle.

"Dr. Hale," she said, choosing her words carefully, "have you shared this story with the reenactors? Do they know about the details?"

Dr. Hale smiled, his expression both proud and sly. "Some do, of course. Edwin, Lady Isolde, and Eleanor—those who have been part of the reenactments the longest. They've all heard the tale, even if it's only in fragments. They see it as a bit of theatre, a dark legend to add spice to the festivities. But... I wonder if some took it more to heart."

Elise felt a chill as she considered his words. If the reenactors saw themselves as heirs to this history, it was possible that one of them had decided to use the cursed chalice not as a prop, but as a means of settling their own feuds.

Dr. Hale continued, "You see, Detective, in this castle, history doesn't stay buried. It rises to the surface, especially when passions run high. For some, reenacting history is a way of reconnecting with their heritage. For others, it's a chance to finally settle old scores."

"Do you think Gareth's death was connected to this story?" Elise asked, watching Dr. Hale's reaction.

His gaze turned solemn. "I think Gareth may have represented, to some, the threat that Lord Robert once did—a figure who clashed with others' ideals, a man who forced those around him to choose between loyalty and betrayal. And I imagine he became the target of someone who thought that history should repeat itself."

Elise shivered, feeling the weight of the legend pressing down on her. "This chalice," she said. "It's more than just a prop for some of them, isn't it?"

"Far more," Dr. Hale agreed. "It's a symbol of fate and consequence. And to those who truly believe in the castle's curse, it is the ultimate test of loyalty. They see it as a way to settle grievances, to decide who is worthy of this place and who is not."

Elise thanked Dr. Hale and made her way back through the castle, her mind filled with a renewed urgency. Gareth's murder wasn't merely the result of a feud—it was part of a ritualized vendetta, a twisted echo of Langford Castle's past. The person who poisoned him had drawn inspiration from a centuries-old legend, casting themselves as an avenger of the castle's honour.

And as she walked through the silent hallways, Elise knew she was getting closer to the truth. Somewhere within the reenactment group, someone had revived Langford Castle's darkest chapter, using its cursed symbols and legends to justify an act of murder.

The poisoned chalice was more than a weapon—it was a message, one that echoed across generations, whispering of betrayal, revenge, and the ghosts of the past that would not rest.

Elise had no intention of letting that message go unanswered. She would uncover the hand that had wielded the poison, and she would ensure that Langford Castle's cursed legacy ended here.

Chapter 15: Whispers in the Walls

Elise moved through Langford Castle's winding corridors, her mind heavy with the weight of the poisoned past Dr. Hale had revealed to her. She knew now that Gareth's death was more than an isolated act of vengeance—it was part of something older, darker, woven into the very stones of Langford Castle. The reenactment group, with its complicated web of rivalries and alliances, seemed to be hiding secrets that went far beyond friendly competition or historical passion. She could feel it, a chill in the air, as though the castle itself whispered to her.

As she passed through the eastern wing, Elise paused, hearing voices coming from a nearby chamber. The door was slightly ajar, and the faint sounds of hushed conversation drifted out. She could make out the murmured tones of two people, though their words were indistinct. Something about their secrecy pricked her instincts, and she moved closer, positioning herself against the wall to listen without being seen.

"—he was reckless. I told him that bringing it up in public was a mistake," a male voice whispered, his tone laced with frustration.

A woman responded, her voice a tense murmur. "It's done now. There's no changing that. But he should've known better. We all agreed not to involve anyone outside."

Elise held her breath, leaning in closer. The conversation seemed loaded with implication, as though the speakers were hiding something much larger than a mere disagreement over Gareth's behaviour.

"The tradition exists for a reason," the man continued, his voice taut. "Our families... we have obligations to the past. If Gareth couldn't respect that, then he didn't belong with us."

The woman's voice softened, almost as if pleading. "But it didn't have to end this way. We could have found another way to... to control him. Now it's spiralling."

Elise's mind raced as she absorbed their words. A tradition, obligations to the past, control—this was far more organized than she'd realized. The reenactors weren't just playing parts in a historical drama; they were following some twisted code, one that seemed bound to ancient grievances and demands.

"People are asking questions," the man continued, his voice dropping lower. "Elise Morrigan is too close, and I don't trust her not to dig deeper. She's not going to stop until she understands."

The woman sighed, her voice edged with anxiety. "We need to be careful. If she finds out about the Oathkeepers..."

Elise felt a chill run down her spine. The Oathkeepers. She repeated the word silently, her mind racing to understand. It sounded like the name of an organization or a society, something clandestine, existing beneath the surface of the reenactment group. The term held a strange weight, as though it were connected to an ancient vow or duty—perhaps to protect the honour of the families involved or uphold certain legacies.

The woman continued, her voice a quiet murmur. "If word gets out that the Oathkeepers were involved in Gareth's death... we'll lose everything we've built. We're meant to be guardians, not... executioners."

"We didn't kill him," the man hissed defensively. "He brought this on himself. We only intended to maintain the integrity of the group, to protect what's ours. He forced our hand."

Elise felt a cold dread settle over her as their words confirmed her suspicions. The Oathkeepers were no mere society—they were enforcers, a secretive order within the reenactors who believed they were responsible for upholding their families' twisted traditions. Bound by history and duty, they seemed willing to go to any length to maintain control over Langford Castle's legacy, even if it meant removing those who threatened their way of life.

THE POISONED CHALICE 75

The woman spoke again, her voice barely above a whisper. "We'll meet tomorrow night, then. The others will expect it, especially after all this... mess. We'll discuss what to do about Elise Morrigan."

Elise's heart pounded as she realized the implication. Not only had they discussed Gareth's death, but now they were actively plotting to prevent her from uncovering the truth. She waited a moment longer, listening as their footsteps faded down the hall, and then slipped away, her mind racing.

Elise moved quickly, weaving through the castle's labyrinthine passages, her mind a storm of thoughts. The Oathkeepers weren't just reenactors. They were guardians of a secret society, bound by a shared belief that the history of Langford Castle was theirs to protect—and police. Gareth's murder had been, in their eyes, justified, an act carried out in the name of maintaining control over the "integrity" of their court.

The implication was chilling. Gareth had been seen as a threat, someone who refused to fall in line with their vision of Langford's traditions. His death was, in their twisted view, a consequence of his defiance, a sentence handed down by a modern-day court of medieval enforcers.

Elise's mind raced as she considered her next move. She had to find proof of the Oathkeepers' involvement, evidence that would expose them for what they were. Their control over the group was too entrenched to rely on mere accusations. She needed something tangible, something undeniable.

The hidden chamber she'd uncovered earlier came to mind. She suspected that the Oathkeepers' activities extended beyond the conversations she'd overheard. If they had taken oaths, if they had left behind any trace of their meetings or their plans, it might be hidden there, among the artifacts and symbols that had once bound them to Langford Castle's blood-stained past.

That night, Elise returned to the hidden chamber, moving carefully through the silent castle until she reached the concealed staircase. Her flashlight illuminated the rough stone walls as she descended, her pulse quickening with every step. She pushed open the heavy wooden door at the bottom, the scent of dust and ancient air filling her senses as she entered the chamber.

This time, Elise searched more thoroughly, her eyes scanning the room for anything she might have missed in her initial inspection. She moved to the shelves filled with relics, examining each item carefully, looking for any hidden compartments or documents.

In a drawer beneath the main table, she found a stack of parchment, old but clearly handled recently. She lifted the top sheet, her breath catching as she read the first lines:

"We, the Oathkeepers of Langford, pledge ourselves to the preservation of our history and the protection of our heritage. We are bound by blood and legacy, sworn to uphold the ancient codes and defend the honour of our kin."

Elise turned the pages slowly, her pulse pounding. Each line detailed the creed of the Oathkeepers, written in a formal, archaic style that resembled a medieval oath. The document described their mission—to maintain Langford Castle's history, to ensure that those who dishonoured its legacy would be dealt with accordingly. It was a pact, one that had likely been made generations ago and handed down to the present members.

She continued reading, and her stomach turned as she found a section outlining the "Rite of Judgment," a method of dealing with those who were deemed a threat to the group's ideals. The rite involved using symbols, tokens, and, chillingly, the cursed chalice itself as a tool for dispensing "justice."

A passage near the end of the document caught her eye, its words written in darker ink, as though recently added:

THE POISONED CHALICE

"The wayward knight has defied the court, choosing pride over loyalty. His fate is sealed by his own actions, and his end shall serve as a warning to those who would disrupt the sanctity of our order. Let the chalice remind them of the price of betrayal."

Elise's heart sank as she recognized the reference to Gareth. They had deemed him the "wayward knight," someone who had overstepped their invisible boundaries, and they had used the chalice—a symbol of their ancient justice—to punish him. The Oathkeepers had truly revived the twisted code of their ancestors, casting themselves as judge, jury, and executioner.

Armed with this knowledge, Elise knew what she had to do. She would confront Edwin, Isolde, and Eleanor—those she suspected were at the heart of this secret society. But she would not go unprepared. She carefully tucked the documents into her coat, determined to keep them hidden until she could bring them to the authorities.

As she left the hidden chamber, Elise felt the weight of Langford Castle's secrets pressing down on her. The Oathkeepers had concealed their actions behind tradition, using history as a shield for murder. But she would shine a light on their dark legacy, exposing the truth they'd guarded for centuries.

The whispers of Langford Castle's walls would soon give way to justice.

Chapter 16: Masks of Honour

As Elise pored over the final pieces of her investigation, a disturbing realization began to crystallize. The reenactment group was more than a gathering of people passionate about history—it was a stage, and each participant wore their role like a mask, blending character and reality in ways that had obscured the truth. And no one, it seemed, had played their role more convincingly than Gareth.

Throughout her interviews, Elise had heard Gareth described as an uncompromising purist, a man who lived by a strict code of honour, devoted to embodying the chivalric values of medieval knighthood. But the more she investigated, the clearer it became that Gareth's ideals were less about preserving history than about controlling those around him. Beneath the armour of "Sir Gareth" lay a man whose ambitions ran deeper—and darker—than anyone had guessed.

Elise returned to the belongings she'd taken from Gareth's quarters, determined to piece together the man behind the mask. Alongside his journal, filled with obsessive notes on knightly codes, battle tactics, and grudges against nearly every member of the group, she discovered a folder of documents. Among them were letters he'd written—unsent letters that revealed a side of Gareth no one had seen.

In one letter, addressed to Edwin, Gareth's words were dripping with resentment:

"You wear the title of lord like it's a game, while I am the one who upholds the true spirit of our order. You compromise, bend to the whims of the weak. I would see Langford restored to its former glory, not tarnished by the likes of you."

Another letter to Lady Isolde revealed a chilling attempt at manipulation:

"You speak of honour and nobility, yet you turn a blind eye to those who sully our traditions. Perhaps you don't understand what's at stake, Isolde. But mark my words—I do. And I will not allow you to undermine what I have built here."

As Elise read further, she found hints of threats, veiled references to secrets Gareth held over his fellow reenactors. In one particularly disturbing letter, Gareth hinted that he had "evidence" of Lady Eleanor's financial troubles, implying he could ruin her reputation if she refused to support his vision for the group. The mask of "Sir Gareth" had not been about honour—it had been about power, a way to impose his will upon others under the guise of noble purpose.

The letters painted a damning picture. Gareth's commitment to "authenticity" and "honour" had been a convenient guise for a much darker agenda. He had wielded his knowledge of the group's secrets like a weapon, using his influence to control and manipulate those around him, pushing them to align with his ideals or suffer the consequences.

Elise's mind reeled as she realized how deeply Gareth's ambitions had run. He had positioned himself as a moral authority within the group, casting judgment on those he saw as threats to his control. And with the hidden society of the Oathkeepers enforcing an even older, darker code, it was no wonder tensions had reached a breaking point.

Determined to learn more about Gareth's true intentions, Elise sought out Edwin, who she found in a small reading room, his face drawn with exhaustion and suspicion. She wasted no time.

"Edwin, I need you to tell me about Gareth's role here— not just as a knight, but as someone who held sway over the group," she began, her tone leaving no room for evasion. "I've found letters—threats he made against you, Isolde, and Eleanor. He was far from the noble knight he claimed to be."

Edwin's face paled, his jaw tightening as he looked away. "Gareth... yes, he liked to think of himself as some kind of enforcer. He was relentless in his views, and if you didn't agree, he'd find ways to... remind you of his influence."

"So, he was blackmailing people?" Elise pressed, wanting to hear it directly from someone who'd experienced Gareth's machinations.

Edwin nodded slowly, his expression grim. "Yes, in his own way. He would bring up things from our past, personal matters, and hint that he'd 'leak' them to the group if we didn't fall in line. He'd imply that we weren't worthy of our roles if we didn't support his vision."

"And the Oathkeepers," Elise continued. "Were they aware of his behaviour?"

Edwin's gaze shifted, a flicker of fear in his eyes. "The Oathkeepers... were supposed to protect our traditions, our families' legacies. But Gareth twisted that, too. He used them to give weight to his demands, turning the Oathkeepers into his enforcers. It was as though he believed he alone understood what Langford needed, and he made sure we knew that defying him would come at a cost."

Elise let his words settle, the picture of Gareth's manipulative power now fully coming into view. He hadn't just been playing the part of a knight; he'd assumed the role of a feudal lord, ruling through fear and intimidation, seeing himself as the last true guardian of Langford's honour.

After leaving Edwin, Elise sought out Lady Eleanor. She found her in a quiet corner of the garden, her usual calm demeanour replaced by a haunted look. When Elise brought up Gareth's threats, Eleanor sighed heavily, her gaze distant.

"Gareth was... obsessed with keeping everyone in line," she admitted. "He believed he knew what was best for Langford, but it wasn't honour he wanted—it was control. He despised anyone who didn't live up to his vision. For him, the reenactment was more than a game. It was an opportunity to wield the power he thought his ancestors deserved."

"Did you ever feel afraid of him?" Elise asked gently.

Eleanor hesitated, her gaze dropping. "At times, yes. He could be cruel, Detective. He would remind me of my family's past, hinting that

THE POISONED CHALICE

81

my family's position in the group was... contingent on my loyalty to him. He wanted me to keep the peace, but only if it meant aligning with him."

As Elise listened, she began to understand the extent of Gareth's influence. He had not only cast himself as a protector of Langford's history but had taken it upon himself to decide who was worthy and who was not. His threats, his manipulation, his use of the Oathkeepers as pawns—all of it had been part of his grand plan to maintain control.

Elise returned to her quarters, sifting through her notes. She had enough evidence now to understand why someone might have wanted Gareth dead. He had gone too far, crossing lines that even those bound by ancient oaths could not tolerate. The Oathkeepers may have been a society devoted to tradition, but Gareth had exploited them, forcing their hand.

It was likely that one of his rivals, one of those he had bullied or manipulated, had finally taken matters into their own hands. The poison in the chalice, the echo of Langford's cursed past, had been their way of stripping him of the power he had wielded so ruthlessly.

Elise gathered her evidence, determined to confront the group. The time had come to unmask the Oathkeepers, to expose their twisted code and the part they had played in Gareth's death.

Later that evening, she convened the reenactors in the Great Hall, her voice ringing out with authority as she addressed them.

"Tonight, I'm here to reveal the truth about the man you all knew as Sir Gareth," she began, her gaze sweeping over the assembled group. "He wore his knightly honour like armour, but beneath it, he was a man who used threats, blackmail, and fear to hold sway over this group. He exploited the very traditions he claimed to protect."

A ripple of shock and fear passed through the crowd as Elise continued.

"He twisted the Oathkeepers' ideals to serve his own ends, using your oaths to enforce his control. And he did it because he believed himself to be the only one worthy of ruling this court."

She looked pointedly at Edwin, Isolde, and Eleanor, watching as the weight of her words settled over them.

"But someone among you saw through his charade," she said, her voice low and steady. "Someone knew that Gareth's mask of honour hid his darker ambitions. And they decided to take matters into their own hands, using the very poison that haunted Langford's past to end his tyranny."

The room was silent, each reenactor's face pale as they absorbed the truth. Gareth's death had been no mere accident; it was the culmination of years of manipulation, of a man's attempt to control a legacy that was not his to wield.

Elise looked around the hall, her voice firm. "Gareth's death was a crime—but it was a crime born of secrets, lies, and fear. It is time to end the masks of honour, to reveal the truth behind the traditions that have cast a shadow over Langford for centuries."

With the unmasking of Gareth's ambitions, Elise knew that the truth would finally bring Langford Castle's twisted history to light, setting its people free from the burdens of the past. The court, and the Oathkeepers within it, would have to confront the consequences of their silence and complicity, and finally lay to rest the ghost of the poisoned chalice.

Chapter 17: A Fateful Duel

Elise sat in the shadowed recess of the Great Hall, flipping through last year's records of the reenactment. Buried in the notes was a brief but telling account of an incident that had occurred during one of their staged duels—a mishap that, to an outsider, might have seemed like an unfortunate accident but, as Elise had learned, had deeper implications.

According to the report, the duel had taken place between Gareth and Edwin, each of them cast in the roles of knight and lord, a ritual duel meant to demonstrate loyalty and honour. However, the contest had quickly escalated into something far more intense, revealing fractures within the group and a dark undercurrent of resentment. The duel had ended with Gareth sustaining a deep cut along his arm, an injury that could have been far worse had Lady Eleanor not intervened and called for a stop to the fight.

Intrigued, Elise sought out Lady Eleanor, who she suspected might offer a more personal account of what had happened. She found her in the castle gardens, her hands clasped together as she looked out over the flower beds, lost in thought.

"Lady Eleanor," Elise greeted, watching as the woman turned with a faint smile. "I wanted to ask you about last year's duel between Gareth and Edwin."

Eleanor's smile faded, her gaze dropping to the ground. "That was... not one of our better moments," she admitted softly. "It started as a simple demonstration, but it became clear that Gareth and Edwin were using it as an opportunity to... settle scores."

"What kind of scores?" Elise pressed gently.

Eleanor sighed, her expression troubled. "Gareth had been challenging Edwin's authority for months. He saw Edwin as a weak leader, too willing to compromise, too hesitant to enforce the standards Gareth believed were essential. Gareth thought of himself as the true knight of our court, and he saw Edwin as an unworthy lord."

"And Edwin?" Elise asked, noting the tension in Eleanor's face.

"Edwin was... resentful of Gareth's constant challenges. He tolerated it, but that duel was his breaking point. They both had points to prove, and I think neither of them was willing to back down."

Eleanor hesitated, glancing away before continuing. "During the duel, Gareth taunted Edwin, calling him 'soft' and unfit to lead. He accused Edwin of desecrating the court's traditions, saying that if Langford's legacy was to be protected, it would be by his hand, not Edwin's. The tension was... palpable."

Elise leaned in, watching Eleanor closely. "And then what happened?"

Eleanor swallowed, her expression grim. "Edwin retaliated, calling Gareth a zealot. He said that Gareth was blinded by his own arrogance, unable to see that his so-called 'honour' was nothing more than an excuse to control everyone else. The exchange got heated, and Gareth struck harder, abandoning the choreography they'd practiced. They weren't duelling anymore—they were fighting."

She closed her eyes, as if reliving the moment. "Gareth lunged with more force than he should have, and Edwin countered with a move that... well, it was dangerous, even with dulled blades. Gareth's arm was cut, and he was bleeding badly. I stepped in to stop them, but by then, the damage had been done."

Elise processed this new information. "Did the incident affect their relationship afterward?"

Eleanor nodded slowly. "It did. Gareth saw Edwin's actions as proof that he was unfit to lead. He called Edwin a traitor to Langford's ideals, and he made it clear that he no longer respected him as lord of the court. The rift between them grew, and it cast a shadow over the entire group. We all felt it."

"Did it create tensions with others in the group as well?" Elise asked, already suspecting the answer.

THE POISONED CHALICE

Eleanor nodded. "Yes. Isolde took Gareth's side, though quietly, believing he was the one who upheld the true essence of our reenactment. Edwin, meanwhile, found support in those who saw Gareth's extremism as a threat to the harmony of the group. By the time this year's reenactment began, there were... factions, even if no one spoke of them openly."

Elise thanked Eleanor and made her way to find Edwin. She located him in the castle's armoury, polishing one of the many swords used in the reenactments. The dim lighting cast shadows over his face, and he looked up as she entered, his expression guarded.

"Detective," he greeted, his tone wary. "Is there something you need?"

"Yes, Edwin," Elise replied, her voice firm. "I wanted to ask you about the duel last year between you and Gareth. I understand it went beyond the bounds of performance."

Edwin stiffened, his jaw tightening. "Yes. That duel... it got out of hand."

"Eleanor told me that Gareth taunted you, questioned your ability to lead," Elise continued, watching him closely. "And that you responded in kind."

Edwin let out a bitter laugh. "Taunted is putting it mildly, Detective. Gareth believed he was the only one worthy of preserving Langford's legacy, and he didn't hide his disdain for anyone who didn't share his rigid views. He accused me of being unworthy, of 'betraying' the castle's ideals. And yes, I pushed back. I told him that his so-called 'honour' was nothing more than a convenient excuse to play tyrant."

"Did you ever want to see him gone?" Elise asked directly, her voice unyielding.

Edwin looked away, his fingers tightening around the hilt of the sword he was polishing. "I won't lie to you, Detective. There were times when I wished he would leave, when I was tired of his constant judgment and accusations. But I never wanted him dead. Gareth... he was a difficult man, but I respected his commitment, even if I didn't agree with it."

Elise noted the mix of frustration and resignation in Edwin's voice. The duel had clearly been a turning point, a moment when their roles had bled into reality, exposing the fractures that lay beneath the surface. Gareth had seen himself as the true knight of Langford, and anyone who threatened that image—especially Edwin—had become a target.

Leaving Edwin in the armoury, Elise sought out Lady Isolde, who had been Gareth's closest ally. She found her in the castle library, surrounded by dusty volumes and ancient scrolls.

"Lady Isolde," Elise greeted, watching as the woman looked up, her gaze calm but wary.

"Detective Morrigan," she replied. "What brings you here?"

"I wanted to discuss last year's duel between Gareth and Edwin," Elise began, her tone measured. "I understand you supported Gareth in his belief that he was upholding the true spirit of the reenactment."

Isolde's expression turned steely. "Gareth was... uncompromising, yes, but he believed in something real. Edwin's approach was too lenient, too focused on appeasing everyone. Gareth felt that if we were going to embody Langford's history, we needed to do it with conviction."

"Even if that meant challenging others?" Elise pressed.

Isolde nodded, her gaze unwavering. "Yes. Gareth believed that the reenactment wasn't just a pastime—it was a way to honour the past. He felt that any deviation from that was a betrayal of Langford's legacy. I respected that about him, even if others saw it as arrogance."

"Did you ever feel that his ambition was dangerous?" Elise asked.

Isolde's gaze flickered. "Gareth was intense, yes, but he was also driven by a desire for authenticity. He held himself to a high standard and expected the same from others. If that was dangerous, it was only because others couldn't live up to it."

THE POISONED CHALICE

As Elise left the library, she pieced together the fragments of that fateful duel, understanding now that it had been more than just a performance gone wrong. It was a clash of ideals, a moment when the boundaries between role and reality had collapsed, leaving raw resentments in their wake.

The duel had been a turning point, one that fractured the group, creating alliances and enmities that had simmered over the past year. Gareth had become a divisive figure, and the duel had only solidified the divide. His unyielding belief in his own righteousness had painted him as both a champion of honour and a tyrant, depending on whom you asked.

Elise now saw how Gareth's death was rooted in that night. The duel had exposed the fractures in the group, setting them on a path toward betrayal, manipulation, and ultimately murder. In challenging Edwin's authority, Gareth had inadvertently sown the seeds of his own demise, forcing those around him to take sides, to either support his vision or to resist it.

Gareth's death was no mere accident or outburst of violence; it was the culmination of a year-long conflict, one that had blurred the lines between honour and vengeance, between role and reality.

And as Elise considered her next steps, she knew that in exposing the truth, she would be tearing away the masks each of them wore, revealing the hidden motives that lay beneath their feudal titles and knightly vows. The court's charade was coming to an end, and the real battle for Langford Castle's legacy was about to begin.

Chapter 18: The Chalice and the Crown

The sun was setting as Elise uncovered yet another dark chapter in Langford Castle's history. In her ongoing search for answers, she had come across an old ledger buried deep within the castle's archives. Bound in cracked leather and nearly crumbling with age, the ledger seemed to have been untouched for centuries, its pages filled with carefully written entries in faded ink.

She opened it cautiously, flipping through lists of supplies, names, and descriptions of events that seemed innocuous at first. But as she turned further, she noticed a recurring entry: The Chalice. Each mention of it was accompanied by names and dates, along with brief notes that sent a chill through her.

One of the earliest entries was dated 1456:

"Sir Rowland de Grey, found in treason, was made to drink from the chalice. None shall speak of him again, and his titles and holdings shall be returned to Langford."

Elise's fingers tightened on the page as she read the entry again, understanding its implications. The chalice was not simply an artifact or a legend—it had been used as a weapon, a grim tool in the castle's brutal history. Those who defied Langford's ruling family, who were accused of betrayal or treachery, were forced to drink from the chalice as a punishment, their deaths attributed to fate or, more chillingly, as "proof" of their guilt. The poisoned chalice was a symbol of retribution, an execution disguised as a medieval trial.

As she continued reading, Elise uncovered other entries, each marking the death of a figure deemed a rival or a threat. The language was cold, detached, but the meaning was clear: the chalice had been wielded as a silent weapon, a means to eliminate those who dared to question or defy the Langford line.

Another entry from 1512 read:

THE POISONED CHALICE 89

"Lady Agnes, who spoke against the marriage alliance, was given the chalice. Let her fate be a warning to those who would disrupt the order of Langford."

The more she read, the clearer it became that the chalice had been more than just a tool of punishment—it was a statement of power. Those who drank from it were condemned not only to die, but to die in disgrace, their legacies erased from memory, their names never spoken again. It was a deliberate erasure, a way to consolidate power by removing any trace of opposition.

The ledger's final entries were even more disturbing, as they indicated the chalice's use right up until the late 17th century, after which it had seemingly vanished. There was no record of the chalice being used after that time, and Elise could only imagine that the castle's occupants had decided it was best left hidden, its history fading into legend to preserve the family's reputation.

As she closed the ledger, Elise's mind raced with the implications. This ledger was a dark chronicle of power plays, betrayals, and quiet executions, all centered around one object: the poisoned chalice. Its presence in Gareth's death wasn't just a symbolic gesture—it was a re-enactment of the castle's darkest tradition.

It was no wonder that the Oathkeepers, the secret society bound to Langford's traditions, had clung to the chalice as a means of "justice." They saw themselves as heirs to this grim legacy, enforcers of a twisted code that had long since lost any claim to honour. Gareth, in their eyes, had been a threat to the "order" they were sworn to protect, and they had chosen to eliminate him in the same way their ancestors had dealt with rivals in centuries past.

Elise was still deep in thought when she heard footsteps approaching. She quickly closed the ledger and slipped it into her bag, glancing up to see Lady Isolde standing in the doorway, her expression unreadable.

"Detective Morrigan," Isolde greeted, her tone cool. "I was told I might find you here."

"Lady Isolde," Elise replied, her own tone guarded. "Is there something I can help you with?"

Isolde stepped into the room, her gaze drifting over the dusty shelves as though searching for something she'd lost. "I've come to see if you've made any progress in your... investigation," she said carefully.

Elise studied her for a moment, wondering how much Isolde already knew. "I have," she replied evenly. "I've discovered quite a bit about the history of this place—and the role the poisoned chalice played in it."

A flicker of something crossed Isolde's face—perhaps surprise, or fear. But she masked it quickly, her expression returning to one of polite interest.

"So, you've learned about the old stories," she said, her tone dismissive. "A bit of dark history to spice up the castle's reputation, nothing more."

"It's more than that, isn't it?" Elise pressed, watching her reaction closely. "The chalice wasn't just a symbol. It was used as a method of execution, a way to deal with those who were seen as a threat to the ruling family. And Gareth... he wasn't the first to die by it."

Isolde's jaw tightened, and for a moment, Elise thought she might deny it. But then her shoulders sagged slightly, and she looked away.

"Gareth was... difficult," she admitted quietly. "He had a way of pushing people, of creating enemies. He thought he was upholding some kind of noble ideal, but in reality, he was trying to control everyone around him."

"And you decided to handle him the same way your ancestors handled their rivals?" Elise asked, her tone hard.

Isolde's gaze sharpened, her eyes flashing with defiance. "It wasn't that simple, Detective. Gareth threatened to destroy everything we'd

THE POISONED CHALICE   91

built here. He saw himself as the last true knight, the only one worthy of preserving Langford's history. He didn't care about the rest of us."

"So, you and the Oathkeepers decided to remove him," Elise said, her voice cold. "You chose to use the chalice, just as it was used centuries ago—to rid yourselves of a problem without leaving a trace."

Isolde's expression turned stony. "Gareth chose his fate. He was warned. He was told to stop, to respect the traditions we hold sacred. But he refused."

Elise took a step forward, her gaze unyielding. "And who decided that he was a threat? Who among you made the choice to bring the chalice back into use, to treat this reenactment as if it were a medieval court?"

Isolde hesitated, her composure cracking for the first time. "We all did. Edwin, Eleanor... even I. Gareth forced our hand, Detective. He pushed us until we had no choice."

Elise shook her head, feeling a chill settle over her. "You had a choice, Isolde. But instead, you revived an ancient, twisted tradition and used it to justify murder. This isn't a medieval court. You aren't knights, or nobles, or rulers. You're people, and you took a man's life to protect an illusion."

Isolde's face hardened, but her eyes betrayed a flicker of shame. "It may be an illusion to you, Detective, but to us, it's a legacy. We are bound by the past, by the oaths we took. Gareth was the one who blurred the lines. He forced us to take drastic measures."

"And now, you'll have to answer for them," Elise replied, her voice firm. "The truth about the Oathkeepers, about the chalice, about Gareth's death—it will all come to light."

With the ledger as evidence and Isolde's reluctant confession, Elise knew she was close to unravelling the entire conspiracy. The Oathkeepers had believed themselves above the law, protectors of a legacy that was little more than a veil for cruelty and manipulation.

The chalice had been a powerful symbol to them, a way of enforcing control, just as it had been centuries ago.

But now, that symbol would be their undoing. The mask of honour they'd worn would be torn away, exposing the twisted ambitions and loyalties that had led to Gareth's death.

As she left the archive, Elise felt a sense of grim satisfaction. The Oathkeepers had tried to hide behind history, but in the end, their poisoned past would condemn them.

Chapter 19: The Maze of Deception

Elise felt she was nearing the truth. The discovery of the ledger detailing the poisoned chalice's grim history had brought her closer to understanding the twisted motivations behind Gareth's murder. But there was still a missing piece—how the chalice had been poisoned without raising suspicion among the reenactors. The answer came unexpectedly that afternoon, from the castle's blacksmith, a grizzled man named Tom Weaver, who had been working with the reenactors for years.

Elise found Tom in his workshop, a small, darkened space filled with the scent of hot metal and soot. Tools of all sizes lined the walls, and the dim light glinted off an array of weapons, armour, and other props he had crafted for the reenactments. As Elise approached, Tom looked up from his work, his face wary but polite.

"Detective Morrigan," he greeted, wiping his hands on a cloth. "To what do I owe the visit?"

"I have a few questions about the props you made for the reenactment group," Elise began, choosing her words carefully. "I understand you were responsible for many of the items they use in their performances."

Tom nodded, his gaze steady. "That's right. I make the armour, weapons, even some of the more... ornate pieces. They like to keep it as authentic as possible, so I do my best to deliver."

"I'm particularly interested in the chalice Gareth used the night he died," Elise continued, watching his reaction closely. "The one with the rubies, tied to the legend of the poisoned chalice. Was that your work?"

Tom's brow furrowed, and he glanced down at his hands, his fingers twisting the cloth. "Aye, I know the chalice you're talking about. I've repaired it a few times over the years. But no, I didn't make it—it's an original piece, passed down through the families here. It's one of those

93

'cursed' artifacts that gives the group a thrill. They like to use it for dramatic effect, you know?"

Elise nodded. "So, the chalice was an antique. But... was it the same chalice used at the feast? The one Gareth drank from?"

Tom hesitated, a flicker of unease crossing his face. "No, Detective, it wasn't. I wasn't supposed to tell anyone, but I think, given what's happened... you should know. A few weeks before the feast, one of the reenactors came to me. They wanted an exact replica of the chalice. Said it was for 'added effect,' something to make the reenactment feel more 'dangerous,' if you can believe it."

Elise felt a surge of adrenaline. "Who was it, Tom? Who asked you for the replica?"

He looked away, rubbing the back of his neck. "It was Edwin. He said the group wanted something indistinguishable from the original, something they could use without putting the real thing at risk. I thought it was strange, but... well, I don't ask questions. They pay me to make things, not question their reasons."

"And did you make it exactly as they wanted?" Elise asked, leaning in.

Tom nodded slowly. "Aye. It was an exact match. I even worked with Eleanor to get the details right, down to the etchings and the ruby inlays. No one would've known the difference. But there's one thing you should know, Detective... the replica I made was hollow, with a hidden compartment in the base. It could be used to slip in... well, anything, really."

Elise's pulse quickened as she absorbed his words. "So, it could have been used to add poison?"

Tom's expression turned grim. "Yes. It wasn't my intention, but it could be used that way. When they asked for it, they didn't mention poison—they only wanted something that looked exactly like the real chalice."

THE POISONED CHALICE

95

"Thank you, Tom. You've been incredibly helpful," Elise said, her voice steady, though her mind was racing. Edwin and Eleanor had gone to great lengths to create a replica chalice, indistinguishable from the original, with a hidden compartment. This meant that the chalice Gareth drank from had likely been switched at the feast, replaced with the poisoned replica that only a few knew about.

Leaving Tom's workshop, Elise headed to the Great Hall, determined to confront Edwin and Eleanor. She found them together, talking in hushed tones, their expressions tight. They fell silent as she approached, exchanging a wary glance.

"Detective," Edwin greeted, forcing a smile. "Is there something we can help you with?"

"Yes, Edwin," Elise replied, her tone sharp. "I spoke with Tom Weaver. He told me about the replica chalice you commissioned."

Eleanor's face paled, and Edwin's smile faded as he stammered, "Replica? I—I thought it would be... safer, Detective. The original chalice is old, fragile."

Elise crossed her arms, her gaze unyielding. "Don't insult my intelligence, Edwin. You didn't have a replica made to 'protect' the original. You had it made so you could use the replica for... other purposes."

Eleanor's hands trembled slightly, but she lifted her chin, meeting Elise's gaze with a defiance Elise hadn't expected. "We only wanted it to add drama, to make the reenactment feel real," she said, her voice steady. "None of us intended for Gareth to die."

"But someone among you did, Eleanor," Elise countered, her tone unrelenting. "The replica chalice was designed to look exactly like the original, but with a hidden compartment. It was made for deception, to hide something dangerous inside."

Edwin's face darkened, his voice low. "Gareth was tearing us apart, Detective. He was relentless, uncompromising, and he would have destroyed everything we built. You can't understand what it was like to have him breathing down our necks, threatening to expose our secrets if we didn't follow his 'vision.'"

"So, you decided to eliminate him?" Elise asked coldly.

Eleanor shook her head, her voice barely a whisper. "We didn't plan to kill him, Detective. We wanted him to feel the weight of the court, to understand the traditions he so often threw in our faces. But things... things went too far."

Edwin's gaze dropped, his hands clenching. "Yes, we thought about it. About teaching him a lesson. But the poison... we never agreed on that. Someone acted on their own."

Elise felt a flash of frustration as they tried to dodge responsibility, but she pressed on. "Someone among you used that chalice to murder Gareth. Whether it was a collective decision or an individual act, the fact remains that you chose to deceive him, to put him in a position of vulnerability. The Oathkeepers may think they're above the law, bound by some ancient code, but that doesn't excuse murder."

Edwin's face hardened, and he finally looked her in the eye. "The Oathkeepers have survived because we've stayed in the shadows, protecting Langford's legacy. Gareth would have destroyed everything. He didn't belong."

Eleanor added, her tone quiet but firm, "We didn't set out to kill him, Detective. We only wanted to keep him from tearing us apart. But now... it seems we've done exactly that."

Elise shook her head, feeling a surge of anger. "You brought this on yourselves, Edwin, Eleanor. You believed that you were above consequence, hiding behind masks of honour and tradition. But in reality, you allowed history to control you, to justify actions you knew were wrong."

The two of them fell silent, their faces etched with guilt and defiance. The facade of loyalty and honour they had clung to had crumbled, revealing the deception and fear that had fuelled their decisions.

THE POISONED CHALICE

Elise stepped back, her voice unyielding. "The truth about Gareth's death will come to light, along with the roles each of you played. You used tradition as a weapon, but now, that very tradition will be your undoing."

As she left the Great Hall, Elise knew that Langford Castle's legacy was on the brink of collapse. The Oathkeepers, who had long believed themselves bound by honour, had twisted that code into something dangerous, allowing their secrets and ambitions to consume them.

The poisoned chalice, once a tool of medieval power plays, had been resurrected as a symbol of deception and betrayal. And now, as the truth unfolded, its dark history would finally be laid bare for all to see.

Chapter 20: The Queen's Gambit

Elise had always found Lady Eleanor an enigma. The woman held herself with a calm authority, exuding a quiet power that seemed to keep the group in balance. Her role as the "queen" of the reenactment court was more than ceremonial; it was the linchpin that held the group's volatile personalities together. But as Elise dug deeper into the dynamics of Langford Castle's reenactments, she began to suspect that Eleanor's influence ran deeper than anyone realized. The recent revelations about the poisoned chalice and the Oathkeepers had raised an unsettling question: could Lady Eleanor, the "queen" of their court, have had her own motives for orchestrating Gareth's downfall?

Elise went back to the records she'd compiled and noted something curious. Over the years, Eleanor had played a significant role in planning the reenactments. She was always involved in the design of key scenes, choosing which historical moments to "revive" and directing how certain participants should portray their roles. While many saw her as a mediator, someone who diffused tensions and preserved harmony, Elise now saw her as something more—a strategist, carefully orchestrating events to maintain her control over the group.

Her suspicions grew when she reviewed past correspondence between Eleanor and Edwin, as well as her own notes from their conversations. Eleanor's letters hinted at her understanding of each member's motivations, resentments, and ambitions. She played a balancing act, subtly influencing the court's power dynamics. And in recent years, her letters revealed her growing frustration with Gareth, whom she saw as a destabilizing force.

Determined to understand her motives, Elise sought out Eleanor in the castle's library, where she often spent her afternoons. She found her seated by the window, leafing through an old tome, her expression serene. But as Elise approached, Eleanor looked up, her smile not quite reaching her eyes.

THE POISONED CHALICE   99

"Detective Morrigan," she greeted, her tone as calm as ever. "What brings you here?"

Elise took a seat across from her, holding Eleanor's gaze. "Lady Eleanor, I've come to ask you about your role in the reenactments. It seems to me that you do more than just keep the peace—you plan these events, sometimes down to the smallest detail."

Eleanor tilted her head slightly, her expression unreadable. "I see myself as a caretaker of Langford's history, Detective. Someone has to ensure that we honour the past with accuracy and respect."

"Is that all it is?" Elise asked, her tone probing. "From what I've seen, your influence extends beyond historical accuracy. You've had a hand in shaping not just the events, but the group itself. And when Gareth became a threat to that balance, it seems you were the one who orchestrated his downfall."

Eleanor's face remained calm, but a flicker of something—perhaps irritation or defiance—passed through her eyes. "Gareth was... difficult. His ideas were noble, but he was inflexible, demanding. He didn't understand the delicate balance required to keep this group together."

"Balance that you control," Elise pointed out. "You positioned yourself as a queen, Eleanor, but it wasn't just a role. You used it to influence people, to shape their actions, and ultimately to protect your own vision of Langford's legacy."

Eleanor's gaze grew steely, and for a moment, Elise saw the full force of the woman's resolve. "Yes, Detective," she admitted quietly. "I kept this group together. I've seen people come and go, seen ambitions flare and fade. But I always ensured that Langford's traditions were preserved, that the court remained whole."

"Even if it meant manipulating people?" Elise asked, her tone unwavering.

Eleanor gave a slight, almost imperceptible nod. "Sometimes, yes. People don't always know what's best for them, especially when they're caught up in their own visions of glory and honour. Gareth was one of those people. He believed he was the only one worthy of Langford's legacy, the only one who truly understood it."

"And you decided he had to go," Elise stated, her voice firm. "You arranged for the replica chalice, knowing it could be used against him. You set the stage for his downfall."

Eleanor's expression softened, though her gaze remained hard. "I did what was necessary, Detective. Gareth was becoming a threat—not only to me but to the entire group. He was sowing discord, creating factions. He would have torn us apart."

"So you poisoned him," Elise said, watching for any reaction.

Eleanor's lips pressed together in a thin line. "No. I never intended for him to die. I only wanted him to feel the weight of his actions, to understand that he wasn't above the traditions he claimed to respect. The poison... I didn't authorize that."

"But you created the conditions for it," Elise replied, her voice cold. "You orchestrated events so that Gareth would be vulnerable, isolated. And then you provided the very tool—the chalice—that someone used to end his life."

Eleanor's gaze faltered for the first time, and she looked down at her hands, clasped tightly in her lap. "Perhaps I did," she admitted softly. "Perhaps I wanted him gone more than I realized. But it wasn't supposed to end like this."

Elise leaned in, her voice low. "Someone used your influence, your plans, to carry out the murder. You may not have poisoned Gareth yourself, but you set him up to fall. And now, you'll have to answer for it."

Eleanor took a deep breath, her expression a mixture of defiance and resignation. "If that's what it takes to protect Langford, so be it. I won't apologize for preserving what matters."

Elise rose, knowing she had uncovered the truth of Eleanor's role. The "queen" of the court had indeed played a ruthless game, using her position to shape the lives and deaths of those around her. She had

THE POISONED CHALICE

orchestrated Gareth's downfall, not with her own hands, but with the careful manipulation of those around her, ensuring that they played their parts in a twisted drama of loyalty and betrayal.

As Elise walked away, she felt the weight of Eleanor's confession. The queen's gambit had cost Gareth his life, and now, Langford Castle's secrets would finally be exposed, leaving its legacy forever changed.

Chapter 21: Broken Vows

Elise had thought she was nearing the end of the investigation, but Langford Castle had one more secret to reveal. Rumours had been swirling among the reenactors, whispers of hidden liaisons and broken promises. As she continued to piece together Gareth's life and influence within the group, she uncovered a new scandal—a tangled web of passion, betrayal, and vengeance, with Gareth right at its center.

Elise first heard of the affair from Tom Weaver, the castle's blacksmith, who seemed to know more about the reenactors' personal lives than they likely realized. She ran into him in the courtyard as he tended to a set of swords, his gaze sharp despite the casual way he greeted her.

"Detective," Tom said, a knowing smile tugging at his lips. "I hear you've been digging deep. But you might want to look a little closer at our 'Sir Gareth' and his, shall we say, extracurricular activities. He didn't exactly live by his knightly code."

Elise arched an eyebrow, sensing he was holding back more than just idle gossip. "What are you getting at, Tom?"

Tom chuckled, shaking his head. "Let's just say Gareth was fond of a certain... participant, someone already spoken for. You didn't hear it from me, but not everyone in the group was thrilled about the 'knight' and his secret conquests."

After pressing him further, Elise finally got a name: Isolde. Her initial shock turned to grim understanding as Tom revealed what many in the group had suspected—that Gareth and Isolde had been involved in an affair that they'd kept hidden for nearly a year. Isolde, known for her fierce independence, had managed to keep the secret under wraps, but her reputation as Lady Isolde, the dignified noblewoman, had always suggested a life above reproach. Gareth, however, was not nearly as discreet. And now, it seemed, the affair had spilled over into

THE POISONED CHALICE   103

the group's carefully maintained dynamics, creating tensions that simmered beneath the surface.

Determined to get the truth, Elise sought out Isolde. She found her in the gardens, her usual poise replaced with a restless energy, as though she knew her carefully kept secret was about to be exposed.

"Lady Isolde," Elise greeted, her tone sharp. "I think it's time you told me about your relationship with Gareth."

Isolde's face paled, and she looked away, gripping the edge of a stone bench. "What do you mean?"

"You know exactly what I mean," Elise replied, watching her closely. "Gareth and you were more than just allies. You were lovers. And that relationship didn't end quietly, did it?"

Isolde swallowed, her hands shaking slightly. "We were... involved," she admitted, her voice barely above a whisper. "But it was a mistake. Gareth was—he was passionate, intense. I thought... I thought we shared a vision. But I didn't realize how possessive he could be."

Elise raised an eyebrow. "Possessive? How so?"

Isolde looked up, her gaze pained. "Gareth had a way of turning everything into a test of loyalty. He didn't just want me by his side; he wanted me to renounce everyone else, to choose him over the court, over my friendships, even over myself. When I tried to end it, he... he didn't take it well."

"Did he threaten you?" Elise asked, her voice steady but firm.

Isolde hesitated, her face twisted with regret. "Not directly, but he made it clear that he wouldn't let me go easily. He would appear at my quarters at odd hours, demanding to know where I'd been, who I'd spoken to. He accused me of betraying him, of turning against him, just like he believed the others had."

"So, he saw himself as the victim?" Elise asked, already sensing the answer.

"Yes," Isolde replied bitterly. "To him, ending our relationship was a betrayal, something unforgivable. He started spreading rumours, hinting that I was untrustworthy, that I was manipulating others. He wanted everyone to think I was the one who'd abandoned him, that I was somehow in the wrong."

Elise watched her, understanding now why the affair would have created enemies. "Did anyone else know about your relationship?"

Isolde sighed, looking away. "Eleanor found out. She confronted me, told me that my involvement with Gareth was dangerous—that it would destabilize the group if it became public. She urged me to end it, to distance myself from him. I took her advice, but by then, Gareth was... fixated. He wasn't willing to let go."

Elise's mind raced as she processed the implications. Eleanor, the "queen" of the court, had known about the affair and had likely seen it as a threat to the court's unity. Isolde, in turn, had tried to break free from Gareth's possessive grip, but Gareth's wounded pride had driven him to lash out, casting suspicion on her and feeding his own narrative of betrayal.

But there was one more piece missing. Elise needed to know how others in the group had reacted to Gareth's possessiveness, and if this scandal had extended beyond Isolde and Eleanor. She sought out Edwin next, knowing he would have a perspective on Gareth's behaviour. She found him in the castle's armoury, where he seemed lost in thought.

"Elise," he greeted, his expression cautious. "You've learned something new, haven't you?"

"Yes, Edwin," she replied bluntly. "I know about Gareth and Isolde's affair. And I know he didn't let it go quietly."

Edwin looked away, his jaw tightening. "Gareth was... difficult, to say the least. He couldn't accept that Isolde had moved on, that she wanted her independence. He believed that she owed him loyalty—total loyalty. And he saw anyone who sympathized with her as a threat."

"Did that include you?" Elise asked, watching his reaction.

THE POISONED CHALICE 105

Edwin nodded, his face hard. "He accused me of trying to undermine him, said that I was turning Isolde against him. He believed I was part of some plot to dethrone him, to steal away what he thought was his 'court.' It was absurd, but Gareth was so convinced of his own narrative that he refused to see reason."

Elise felt the final pieces of the puzzle sliding into place. Gareth had cast himself as a tragic figure, betrayed by those closest to him. His obsession with loyalty, combined with his wounded pride, had driven him to make enemies out of his former friends and allies. Isolde had become a target of his scorn, and Edwin, by extension, had been labelled a traitor.

But Eleanor's role now seemed even more significant. She had known about the affair, seen it as a threat, and likely orchestrated events to remove Gareth as a source of instability. The replica chalice, the Oathkeepers' involvement, the layers of deception—all of it pointed to Eleanor's carefully calculated strategy to rid the court of its disruptive knight, using the scandal of the affair as a catalyst.

As Elise returned to the main hall, she could see how the affair had sown division within the group. Gareth's actions had created a court rife with distrust, resentment, and anger. Isolde had tried to reclaim her freedom, while Edwin had been forced to navigate Gareth's accusations. And Eleanor, seeing the chaos as a threat to her carefully curated control, had taken matters into her own hands.

That night, Elise gathered the reenactors in the Great Hall. She knew that the time had come to reveal the truth of Gareth's death, not just as a murder, but as a culmination of broken promises and shattered loyalties.

"Everyone here played a role in the events that led to Gareth's death," Elise began, her voice resonating through the hall. "Gareth's affair with Isolde, his possessive need for control, and his accusations of betrayal turned this court into a battlefield of secrets and lies."

The group murmured, shifting uncomfortably as Elise continued.

"Eleanor knew about the affair and saw it as a threat to the unity of the court. Edwin and Isolde became targets of Gareth's paranoia, branded as traitors for refusing to bend to his demands. And in the end, Gareth's own arrogance, his refusal to let go, led him to his death."

Eleanor's face was impassive, but her eyes betrayed a flicker of fear. Edwin and Isolde, meanwhile, looked relieved to have the truth finally out, even if it was painful.

"Gareth may have cast himself as a knight, a man of honour," Elise concluded, "but he was no hero. His choices tore apart the court he claimed to protect. And now, the truth has unmasked all of you, revealing the hidden motives and betrayals that fuelled this tragedy."

As the court sat in stunned silence, Elise felt a grim sense of closure. The affair, the poison, the feigned honour—all of it had finally been exposed, shattering the illusion of loyalty that Langford Castle had so carefully preserved.

The court, once bound by secrets, now had no choice but to face the broken vows and bitter truths that lay at its heart. And for the first time, Langford's shadows seemed to lift, leaving only the cold, undeniable reality behind.

Chapter 22: The Shadowed Ritual

Elise was certain she'd uncovered all the secrets Langford Castle held. But another revelation emerged, adding yet another dark layer to the tangled web of loyalty, betrayal, and vengeance that had culminated in Gareth's death. As she pieced together the events of the night before the feast, a new piece of information reached her: some of the reenactors had gathered secretly, performing a ritual that, according to legend, had always ended with the "sacrifice of the traitor."

This final clue came from none other than Elias, Gareth's young and loyal squire. She found him sitting alone in the courtyard, clearly shaken, his eyes shadowed with guilt and anxiety.

"Elise... Detective Morrigan," he began, his voice a whisper, "I need to tell you something. I... I was part of a gathering, a ritual, the night before Gareth... before the feast. I thought it was just going to be another of our reenactments, something to make the experience feel more... real."

Elise felt a chill run through her. "Tell me everything, Elias. Who was there, and what did you do?"

Elias took a shaky breath, glancing around to make sure they were alone before speaking. "Lady Eleanor led the ritual, with Edwin, Isolde, and a few others present. It wasn't uncommon for us to perform certain rites before major reenactments, a way to bond, to remind ourselves of our commitment. But this time, Eleanor told us it was a special ritual, one that honoured Langford's history."

"What kind of ritual?" Elise asked, her voice steady but sharp.

Elias hesitated, his face pale. "It was called 'The Oath of Shadows.' Lady Eleanor said it was an ancient rite that the castle's nobles had once performed, a ceremony to reinforce loyalty and unity among their ranks. But... but it wasn't just about loyalty. She said the rite also marked someone as the 'traitor,' the one who would bear the consequences of betrayal."

Elise's heart pounded as she absorbed this new information. "And who was marked as the traitor?"

Elias looked down, his hands clenched tightly. "Gareth. Eleanor led us through a series of chants, each of us reciting an oath to protect Langford's honour. At the end, she told us that Gareth had strayed from that honour, that his actions had threatened the very soul of the court. She claimed that the ritual was a way to confront him, to give him a chance to renounce his behaviour. But... but there was something ominous about it. She mentioned that in the past, such rituals often ended in the 'sacrifice of the traitor,' a symbolic act to cleanse the group of disloyalty."

Elise felt the weight of his words pressing down on her. "Did Gareth know about this ritual? Was he present?"

Elias shook his head, looking ashamed. "No, he wasn't there. We all... we went along with it because Eleanor told us it was tradition, that it was a way to uphold Langford's legacy. But it felt wrong, Detective. She told us we were protecting the group, but I think... I think she knew exactly what she was doing."

"Elaborate, Elias," Elise pressed. "Do you believe Eleanor intended for Gareth to be... sacrificed?"

Elias swallowed, his voice dropping to a whisper. "She kept talking about the importance of loyalty, of removing those who didn't belong. She said that once we'd named a traitor, it was our duty to protect the court by any means necessary. I thought she was speaking figuratively, but now... now I'm not so sure."

Elise nodded, understanding the full gravity of what Elias was revealing. The ritual wasn't just symbolic; it was a way for Eleanor to mark Gareth, to cast him as the villain in the eyes of the court. Under the guise of tradition, she had laid the groundwork for his downfall, giving the group a moral justification for what would follow.

"Thank you, Elias," she said quietly. "You've done the right thing by coming forward."

THE POISONED CHALICE

109

Leaving Elias, Elise sought out Eleanor, her mind racing with questions. She found her in the castle's chapel, a small, dimly lit room adorned with ancient tapestries and medieval relics. Eleanor was alone, standing near the altar, her expression calm but weary.

"Detective Morrigan," she greeted, her voice barely above a whisper. "I had a feeling you would come to see me."

Elise stepped forward, her gaze hard. "Eleanor, I know about the ritual. The Oath of Shadows, the marking of the 'traitor.' You performed it with the group the night before the feast, knowing that Gareth would be its target."

Eleanor's face remained impassive, but there was a flicker of something in her eyes—defiance, perhaps, or resignation. "Yes, we performed the ritual," she admitted. "It was part of our heritage, a way to preserve the past."

"But it wasn't just a reenactment, was it?" Elise pressed, her voice unyielding. "You knew that the ritual would cast Gareth as a traitor, that it would make him a target. You didn't need to poison him yourself because you'd already laid the foundation for his downfall."

Eleanor's lips pressed together, her gaze dropping to the floor. "Gareth's behaviour was tearing us apart. He believed himself above the rest of us, the sole arbiter of Langford's honour. We couldn't allow that. The ritual was meant to remind us of our commitment to each other, of the sacrifices we were willing to make to protect what we've built here."

Elise shook her head, anger flaring in her chest. "No, Eleanor. It was a twisted manipulation, a way to justify your actions. You led your friends through a ritual that ended in Gareth's death, and you called it tradition. You turned him into a scapegoat, knowing that once he was marked as a traitor, someone would take matters into their own hands."

Eleanor's face remained stoic, but her eyes betrayed a hint of regret. "Perhaps I underestimated the impact of the ritual. I didn't intend for Gareth to die, Detective. I only wanted to remind him—and the others—of the importance of loyalty."

Elise stepped closer, her voice low. "You can tell yourself that, but the truth is that you set him up. You painted him as a traitor, a villain who needed to be purged to protect the court. And someone followed through, turning your ritual into a reality."

For a long moment, Eleanor was silent, her gaze fixed on the flickering candlelight. When she finally spoke, her voice was barely audible. "Maybe... maybe you're right. Maybe I wanted him gone, more than I was willing to admit."

Elise looked at her, feeling a mixture of anger and pity. "You used tradition as a weapon, Eleanor. And in doing so, you destroyed the very court you claimed to protect."

Eleanor met her gaze, a shadow of sorrow in her eyes. "What's done is done, Detective. I cannot undo what happened. But Langford's legacy will endure, even if I have to pay the price for it."

Elise left her in the chapel, feeling the weight of Eleanor's words and the hollow justification behind them. The ritual had been a calculated act, designed to cast Gareth as a traitor and give the group a reason to turn against him. Eleanor had cloaked her intentions in the trappings of tradition, manipulating those around her to fulfil her vision of loyalty and honour.

As Elise stepped into the cold night air, she knew the truth: Gareth's death had been the result of a ritual, a shadowed act that had twisted loyalty into vengeance and sacrifice. And now, with the full story finally revealed, Langford Castle's dark legacy would be laid bare for all to see.

The echoes of the past had guided their hands, but this time, there would be no veil of honour to hide behind.

Chapter 23: Betrayal at the Banquet

As Elise sifted through the final pieces of evidence, she found herself questioning everything she thought she knew about Gareth's death. A pattern of clues had begun to emerge, suggesting that the poisoned chalice might not have been meant for Gareth at all. If true, then Gareth's death was not just a ritualized punishment—it was a tragic mistake.

The revelation came from a new witness, Sarah, one of the castle's kitchen staff who had been responsible for preparing and serving the drinks at the feast. Elise found her in the servants' quarters, her expression anxious as she twisted a handkerchief in her hands.

"Detective Morrigan," Sarah began, her voice shaky. "There's something I should have told you earlier... something about the night of the feast."

Elise sat down beside her, her tone gentle. "Go on, Sarah. Anything you can tell me might be important."

Sarah took a deep breath, her gaze darting around nervously. "When I brought out the chalices, Lady Eleanor specifically instructed me to place the jewelled chalice—the one that matched the cursed chalice—at the head of the table. She told me that it was meant for a special guest, someone of importance, though she didn't say who."

Elise felt a chill settle over her as she absorbed Sarah's words. "So Eleanor intended for the chalice to be used by a specific person?"

Sarah nodded, biting her lip. "Yes, but it didn't end up where she wanted it. I set it at the head of the table as instructed, but during the feast, there was a lot of movement. People were rearranging their seats, toasts were being made... and somehow, Gareth ended up with the chalice."

Elise's mind raced as she processed the implications. If Eleanor had indeed orchestrated the placement of the chalice, it meant that the intended target was likely someone else. But with the chaos of the feast,

Gareth had unknowingly claimed the chalice for himself, becoming an unintended victim of a scheme meant for another.

Leaving Sarah, Elise went over the seating arrangement and who might have been the intended target. With Eleanor's influence over the group and the symbolic weight of the chalice, Elise suspected that the real target was someone whom Eleanor might have seen as a deeper threat—someone she could not control.

Returning to her notes on the group dynamics and alliances, Elise's thoughts circled back to Edwin. As the "lord" of the court, Edwin held authority that Eleanor likely resented or felt threatened by, particularly as Gareth had supported Edwin's leadership. Could it be that Eleanor had meant for the chalice to reach Edwin, eliminating him as an obstacle once and for all?

Seeking clarity, Elise tracked down Edwin in his chambers. His face was drawn with exhaustion, yet he met her gaze steadily as she entered.

"Detective," he greeted, his tone cautious. "What have you found?"

"Eliminating Gareth may not have been the original plan," Elise said, watching his reaction closely. "The poisoned chalice—there's reason to believe it was meant for someone else. Possibly... you."

Edwin's eyes widened, surprise and horror flickering across his face. "Me? Why would someone want me dead?"

"Think about it, Edwin," Elise pressed. "You were the leader of the court, the one responsible for maintaining order. Eleanor viewed you as a threat to her own influence over the group. If she had control over Gareth, removing you would have cleared the way for her authority."

Edwin looked away, processing her words. "I'd heard whispers of discontent, rumours that Eleanor saw me as too lenient, too willing to compromise. But to think she'd go as far as—" He broke off, shaking his head. "It's... difficult to believe."

But Elise could see that the truth was beginning to dawn on him. "During the feast, there was movement, people switching places. Gareth, perhaps unknowingly, ended up taking your seat at the head of

THE POISONED CHALICE

the table. He was always eager to assert his presence, to demonstrate his own form of loyalty. It's possible that in the chaos, he simply took the chalice meant for you."

Edwin's face grew pale as he absorbed her theory. "So, Gareth's death... it was never supposed to happen. Eleanor was aiming for me."

"Yes," Elise replied, her voice low. "Eleanor, or perhaps someone working alongside her. Gareth was marked by the ritual, but the chalice was positioned for a reason—to quietly eliminate a rival."

Elise left Edwin deep in thought and sought out Eleanor, finding her in the library, surrounded by books detailing Langford's history. She looked up as Elise approached, her face guarded.

"Detective," she greeted, her tone cautious. "Is there something else?"

"Yes, Eleanor," Elise replied, her voice firm. "I know the poisoned chalice wasn't meant for Gareth. It was meant for someone you saw as a threat. Someone who, in your eyes, didn't belong in the court."

Eleanor's face betrayed a flicker of surprise, but she quickly composed herself. "What are you implying, Detective?"

"I'm not implying anything. I'm stating a fact," Elise said, her gaze steady. "You orchestrated the ritual, marked Gareth as the 'traitor,' but you arranged for the poisoned chalice to be placed at the head of the table. You knew that seat was meant for someone you couldn't control—Edwin."

Eleanor's lips pressed into a thin line. "Edwin is... weak. He lacks the conviction to lead. I believed he would ruin everything we've worked for."

"So you decided to remove him," Elise said coldly. "You orchestrated the seating, ensured the chalice was placed in his position. But in the chaos of the feast, Gareth took it instead. You caused Gareth's death, Eleanor, whether you intended it or not."

Eleanor's face twisted with a mixture of regret and defiance. "Perhaps I made a mistake. But it was in the service of Langford's legacy. I did what I thought was necessary."

Elise shook her head, anger flashing in her eyes. "You tried to rewrite history to suit your own agenda, manipulating those around you to protect an illusion of power. You used loyalty, tradition, and honour as weapons to justify murder."

Eleanor's voice grew quiet, her gaze dropping. "I acted for the good of the court. Edwin would have weakened us, made us vulnerable."

"But it's over now, Eleanor," Elise replied, her tone final. "You've torn the court apart, sacrificed someone who wasn't even your true target. Langford Castle's legacy is stained not by honour, but by deceit and betrayal."

With Eleanor's scheme exposed, Elise knew the court would no longer see her as a figure of authority. The ritual, the poison, the manipulation—all of it had been laid bare. And as Eleanor stood alone in the library, the shadows of Langford's twisted legacy seemed to close in around her.

Leaving her to confront the consequences of her actions, Elise felt the weight of Langford Castle's secrets lifting. The truth of Gareth's death had finally come to light: a tragic consequence of power plays and betrayal, a story twisted by those who believed themselves protectors of history.

In the end, the court had not been bound by honour but by fear and manipulation, each member trapped in a web of loyalty and deception that had nearly claimed yet another life.

And now, with the shadows receding, Langford's dark legacy would finally be exposed to the light of truth.

Chapter 24: Secrets in the Script

Elise felt close to unravelling the final thread of the conspiracy surrounding Gareth's death. Every new clue revealed another layer of manipulation and deception, but one detail had remained elusive: how had each reenactor's actions been so perfectly orchestrated to result in Gareth's murder? The answer, she realized, lay in the reenactment's carefully crafted script—a script that directed not just the scenes, but the movements, interactions, and even the secrets of each participant.

The script, she learned, was a central part of every reenactment at Langford Castle. Each year, it was meticulously planned by the group's leaders to honour specific historical events and weave in relevant subplots. The script was generally overseen by Lady Eleanor and Edwin, but Elise suspected that someone had taken liberties with it this year, using it as a means to guide Gareth toward his death without raising suspicion.

Elise combed through the records in the castle's archives, looking for previous scripts to see if there had been any recent changes. After hours of searching, she found the current year's script stored in a dusty file. As she read through it, her suspicions were confirmed. This year's reenactment diverged from the traditional layout, including new scenes and character interactions that had not been part of previous years' scripts.

The most striking change was the addition of a "Traitor's Trial," a dramatic confrontation that culminated in a public accusation of betrayal. The script described a climactic moment at the feast where the accused, the so-called "traitor," would be singled out and forced to answer for their actions before the court. The role of the "traitor," as it turned out, had been assigned to Gareth.

Elise's mind raced as she pieced together the implications. The reenactment wasn't merely intended to honour history; it had been designed to corner Gareth, forcing him to play the role of a disgraced knight, marked for punishment. This script, with its pointed scenes and altered interactions, was a trap, each scene subtly reinforcing Gareth's isolation and marking him as the court's scapegoat.

Seeking more insight into how the script might have been manipulated, Elise tracked down Lady Eleanor, who had overseen much of the planning. She found Eleanor in the study, surrounded by documents and books on Langford's history. Eleanor looked up, her face tense as Elise entered.

"Detective Morrigan," she greeted, her voice calm but wary. "To what do I owe this visit?"

Elise took a seat across from her, her tone direct. "I've been reviewing this year's script. It's quite different from previous years, particularly with the addition of the 'Traitor's Trial.' Can you explain why that was included?"

Eleanor's eyes flickered, a brief look of surprise crossing her face before she composed herself. "The Traitor's Trial was meant to heighten the drama, Detective. We wanted to create a scene that embodied Langford's history of loyalty and betrayal. It was symbolic."

"Symbolic," Elise repeated, her tone sceptical. "Or an opportunity to cast Gareth as a villain in front of the entire group, marking him as a target. Did you assign him the role of 'traitor' intentionally, Eleanor?"

Eleanor's expression tightened, and she looked away. "Gareth... insisted on authenticity. He believed he was the only one who truly understood Langford's legacy. I thought assigning him the role would force him to confront his own rigid ideals, to see that honour is a choice we all must make."

"But it was more than that, wasn't it?" Elise pressed. "The script's scenes, the dialogue, the confrontations—all of it was designed to isolate him, to make him believe he'd been betrayed. And in the end, the feast scene would see him accused and punished. You scripted his downfall, Eleanor."

THE POISONED CHALICE   117

Eleanor's face turned stony, but her voice wavered slightly. "I didn't mean for him to die, Detective. The script was a way to control him, to force him to see the limits of his so-called honour. I wanted him to feel the weight of his own actions, to understand that loyalty cannot be demanded—it must be earned."

"But someone took that script and used it to orchestrate his murder," Elise said, her voice cold. "You gave them the perfect setup, a scripted narrative that painted Gareth as a traitor, ensuring that he would drink from the poisoned chalice without question."

Eleanor sighed, a trace of regret in her eyes. "Perhaps... perhaps I went too far. But I was not the only one involved in planning the script. Edwin contributed as well, as did others. We all had a hand in it."

"Who had access to make changes to the script?" Elise asked, her tone sharp.

Eleanor hesitated, then replied quietly, "Edwin and I oversaw the main plot, but the subplots and interactions... I left much of that to Isolde. She wanted to add layers to the performance, to create moments that felt real for each member of the court. I trusted her judgment."

Elise's eyes narrowed as she realized the full extent of the conspiracy. Eleanor had shaped the main script to isolate Gareth, but Isolde had likely layered the scenes with personal motives, reinforcing the betrayal narrative. Together, they had set a trap, each change to the script further tightening the noose around Gareth's neck.

Seeking answers, Elise left Eleanor and sought out Isolde, finding her in the rehearsal hall where props and costumes were stored. She confronted her without preamble.

"Isolde," Elise began, her voice steely, "you altered the script, didn't you? Added scenes and moments to reinforce the idea that Gareth was a 'traitor.' You knew exactly how he would respond to the accusations."

Isolde froze, her gaze sharp and defensive. "I don't know what you're talking about, Detective."

"Don't lie to me," Elise replied, her tone unyielding. "You had access to the script and manipulated it to cast Gareth in the worst possible light. Every encounter, every line—it was all designed to make him feel betrayed, to break his spirit. You may not have poisoned him yourself, but you created the conditions that led to his death."

Isolde's face hardened, and she crossed her arms, a trace of bitterness in her voice. "Fine. Yes, I added scenes. Gareth was arrogant, inflexible. He saw himself as a martyr for Langford's legacy, and I wanted him to see the cost of his actions. But I never intended for him to die."

"Then who did?" Elise asked, her voice cold. "You, Eleanor, Edwin—all of you had a hand in scripting Gareth's downfall. But someone used that script to turn a punishment into a death sentence."

Isolde's face paled, her defiance wavering. "I... I don't know. We all resented him in different ways, but I never expected it to go this far. Eleanor may have led us, but none of us believed Gareth would actually be... sacrificed."

Elise shook her head, feeling a mix of anger and sorrow. "You used tradition and honour to justify your actions, twisting a performance into a death sentence. You made Gareth believe he was the villain, that he'd been betrayed by everyone he trusted. And when he finally drank from the chalice, he did so believing it was his punishment."

Isolde looked down, her expression haunted. "Maybe we did push him too far. Maybe... we all went too far."

As Elise left her, she felt the weight of the truth settle over her. The script had been the silent weapon, carefully crafted and subtly altered to lead Gareth toward his death. Eleanor, Edwin, and Isolde had each played a part, using the reenactment to turn their grievances into a ritualized punishment. They hadn't intended for Gareth to die, but their manipulation had set in motion a tragedy that none of them could stop.

THE POISONED CHALICE   119

Returning to the Great Hall, Elise gathered the group, her voice ringing out as she finally laid bare the truth.

"The script you all followed was designed to cast Gareth as a traitor, to isolate him and break his spirit. Each of you had a role in pushing him to the brink, orchestrating his downfall under the guise of loyalty and tradition. And in the end, someone used that script as a cover for murder."

The room was silent, each member's face reflecting a mixture of guilt, shame, and horror.

"You all wore masks of honour, but those masks hid your true motives—resentment, jealousy, ambition. You called it tradition, but in reality, it was betrayal."

As the court sat in stunned silence, Elise felt a grim sense of resolution. Langford's legacy had been warped by those who claimed to honour it, each reenactor complicit in the twisted drama that had cost Gareth his life.

And now, with the script exposed, they would all face the truth of their actions, leaving the court of Langford Castle shattered by the weight of their own secrets.

Chapter 25: The Final Revelation

The investigation had been a labyrinth of hidden motives, carefully orchestrated roles, and twisted loyalties. But Elise felt she was finally nearing the heart of the conspiracy that had claimed Gareth's life. A fresh lead emerged from an unexpected source: Marcus, the group's designated archer, who had mostly kept to himself throughout the reenactment. Elise had noted his reserved demeanour, his tendency to observe rather than participate in the court's drama. Yet, as she would learn, Marcus had more at stake in Gareth's death than anyone had suspected.

Elise found Marcus practicing his aim in the castle's courtyard, a worn target set up against one of the far walls. She approached him cautiously, and he lowered his bow, his gaze steady as he looked at her.

"Detective Morrigan," he greeted, his tone wary but calm. "What can I do for you?"

"I wanted to ask you about your relationship with Gareth," Elise said, watching him closely. "I've heard you and he had a falling-out. Something to do with the group's funds?"

Marcus's expression tightened, and he looked away, his hands clenching around the bow. "That's an understatement. Gareth and I... we disagreed on a lot of things, but the funds were the final straw."

"Tell me what happened," Elise urged, sensing that Marcus was holding back.

Marcus hesitated, then took a deep breath. "About a year ago, Gareth approached me with a plan to 'restore' the court. He said we needed better costumes, more authentic props, and that it would require a considerable amount of money. I didn't disagree with him on that, but he wanted complete control over the group's funds. He insisted that he alone knew how to spend the money, that his vision would ensure the reenactment's success."

"And you didn't trust him with that responsibility?" Elise asked.

THE POISONED CHALICE
121

Marcus shook his head, his face hardening. "Gareth was passionate, but he was reckless. He wanted to pour money into grand displays, things that weren't sustainable for our budget. When I questioned him, he became defensive, accusing me of trying to undermine him, of being disloyal to Langford's 'legacy.' It wasn't just about money for him—it was about control."

Elise nodded, understanding now why their conflict had grown so intense. "What happened after that?"

"We had a huge argument," Marcus admitted, his voice bitter. "Gareth was furious. He said I was standing in the way of progress, that I didn't understand his vision. He wanted to take the group in a new direction, one that put him at the center of everything. Eventually, he told me he didn't need my support and threatened to remove me from the group entirely if I didn't comply."

Elise raised an eyebrow. "Did you ever consider leaving?"

"I did," Marcus admitted. "But I'd been part of this reenactment for years, long before Gareth showed up. I wasn't about to let him push me out. So I stayed, but we barely spoke after that. I tried to avoid him whenever possible."

Elise watched him carefully, considering the implications. "So, you had a personal grudge against Gareth. A grudge that could have given you a motive to... remove him as an obstacle."

Marcus's eyes darkened, and he shook his head firmly. "No, Detective. I may have resented him, but I would never kill him. I wanted to protect the group, to ensure we didn't waste everything we'd built on Gareth's ambitions. But murder? That's not who I am."

"Then let me ask you this, Marcus," Elise continued, her voice calm but pointed. "Did you know about the ritual the night before the feast? The one where Gareth was marked as the 'traitor'?"

Marcus's jaw clenched, and he nodded slowly. "Yes. I knew about it. Eleanor and a few others approached me, asked me to join. They said it was a symbolic act, something to reinforce the court's loyalty. I didn't want to be involved in their games, but... I was there. I watched as they cast Gareth in that role, marked him as the one who'd strayed from their so-called 'legacy.'"

"Did you feel that the ritual was dangerous?" Elise asked.

Marcus hesitated, then nodded. "It was... unsettling. They all spoke about loyalty and tradition, but there was something darker beneath it. Eleanor especially—she was determined to make Gareth see the error of his ways. I think part of her wanted him gone, but she didn't have the nerve to do it directly."

"So, you believe Eleanor orchestrated the ritual to manipulate others into seeing Gareth as a traitor?" Elise pressed.

Marcus's expression was grim. "Yes. She wanted Gareth to feel isolated, to break him down. She used that ritual to turn the entire group against him, to make him question himself and his place in the court. And it worked. By the end, Gareth was completely alone, surrounded by people who saw him as a threat."

Elise's mind raced as the full picture came into view. The ritual, the altered script, the poisoned chalice—each element had been meticulously arranged to isolate Gareth, to break his spirit and lead him to his death. But now, with Marcus's revelation, Elise could see that Eleanor's manipulation had extended even further, turning Gareth's allies against him and creating an environment in which he was completely vulnerable.

Leaving Marcus, Elise returned to the Great Hall, where she found Eleanor seated alone, lost in thought. This time, there was no hesitation in her approach, no pretence of diplomacy.

"Eleanor," Elise said firmly, her voice echoing in the empty hall. "I know what you did. You manipulated the script, orchestrated the ritual, and turned Gareth's closest allies against him. All to make him feel isolated, to ensure that he would drink from that chalice without question."

THE POISONED CHALICE 123

Eleanor looked up, her face pale but defiant. "I did what was necessary, Detective. Gareth was a threat to everything we've built. He would have torn us apart."

"You used loyalty and tradition as weapons," Elise accused. "You didn't just plan a performance—you arranged for his death, whether you're willing to admit it or not."

Eleanor's face twisted, a mixture of regret and defiance. "Maybe I wanted him gone, Detective. Maybe I believed he would destroy us if left unchecked. But I never intended to kill him. I only wanted to show him the cost of his actions."

"But someone took your plans further," Elise replied, her tone sharp. "Someone used that chalice to turn your punishment into a death sentence."

Eleanor's face fell, and for a moment, she looked truly defeated. "Perhaps... I underestimated the consequences. But I'm not the only one responsible, Detective. Each member of the court had a role in this. We all played our parts."

Elise nodded, her voice firm. "Yes, and now every one of you will have to answer for it."

As she left the hall, Elise felt a sense of finality settle over her. The truth of Gareth's death had finally been exposed: a tragic consequence of ambition, betrayal, and the lengths people would go to in order to protect their power.

Langford Castle's court had been a stage of secrets, each member playing their part in a deadly drama that had ultimately claimed one of their own. Now, with the final revelation laid bare, the court would have to face the truth of their actions, no longer hidden behind masks of loyalty and honour.

The poisoned chalice, the ritual, the script—all of it had been carefully crafted to lead to this end. But in the end, the court of Langford Castle had sacrificed not only Gareth, but also the legacy they had sworn to protect.

Chapter 26: The Keeper's Code

Elise was nearing the end of her investigation, but a nagging sense of unfinished business remained. The circumstances surrounding Gareth's death had been a tangled web of motives, resentments, and betrayals, yet something about the physical logistics of the reenactment still didn't add up. How had the poisoned chalice been swapped without anyone noticing? How had certain people appeared and disappeared so easily during the feast and the preceding days? The answer, it seemed, lay with the castle's keeper, an older man named Alistair Kane, who had dedicated his life to preserving Langford Castle's history.

Alistair was an enigmatic figure, someone who moved in the shadows of Langford, keeping the secrets of the castle with a quiet intensity. Elise found him in the chapel, dusting an old suit of armour with reverent care. He glanced up as she approached, his eyes crinkling in a subtle smile.

"Detective Morrigan," he greeted, his voice gravelly but warm. "I thought you might come looking for me before you were done here."

Elise nodded, watching him closely. "Mr. Kane, I understand that you know the castle's layout better than anyone. And I've heard there may be... hidden passages—tunnels that would allow people to move unseen through the castle."

Alistair chuckled, setting down his cloth. "You'd be right about that. Langford Castle has a rich history, Detective, and with that comes its share of secrets. Tunnels and hidden rooms were often used in times of war or... political intrigue, shall we say. They were built to protect the family, to allow them to escape or to move undetected."

"And these tunnels," Elise continued, "are they still accessible?"

Alistair's gaze grew distant, a spark of something almost mischievous in his eyes. "Most of them, yes. They're not common knowledge, though. Only a few people in the castle know about them, and they're rarely used these days. But I suppose a few of the reenactors

THE POISONED CHALICE   125

might have discovered them over the years. I've seen some of them exploring, poking around in places they shouldn't."

Elise's pulse quickened. "Could one of these tunnels lead to the Great Hall or the quarters near it? Enough to allow someone to move quickly and without being seen?"

Alistair nodded slowly. "Indeed. One of the main tunnels runs from the south wing of the castle, near the Great Hall, all the way to the old stables. It branches off into smaller passageways, some leading to hidden alcoves, others to private rooms."

He paused, his gaze sharpening as he studied Elise. "You're wondering how someone might have used these passages to orchestrate that night, aren't you?"

"Yes," Elise replied, her voice low. "If certain people knew about these tunnels, they could have moved through the castle undetected, swapped the chalice, and avoided being seen during the feast. It would explain how the plan was executed so precisely."

Alistair's expression grew serious. "There is something you should know, Detective. The hidden passages are part of an old tradition, one I'm sworn to protect. We call it 'The Keeper's Code.' The code is not just about maintaining the tunnels—it's about preserving the castle's history, protecting its secrets."

Elise tilted her head, intrigued. "And does that code allow for murder?"

Alistair's gaze was steady, though his eyes held a hint of sorrow. "The Keeper's Code was meant to protect the castle and its inhabitants, not to harm them. But there have been times when the line has blurred, when people believed they were serving a higher purpose by acting in... morally ambiguous ways."

"And you believe that's what happened here?" Elise asked.

Alistair sighed, nodding. "I do. The reenactors are more than players in a historical performance—they are caretakers of the castle's legacy, bound to it in ways they might not even understand. For some, that responsibility becomes a form of obsession. I suspect that someone believed they were fulfilling an ancient duty by removing Gareth, someone they saw as a threat to Langford's honour."

Elise considered his words, a chill settling over her. "So, the tunnels provided them with the means to carry out this twisted sense of duty undetected."

Alistair gave a sombre nod. "Yes. The south wing passage opens into a narrow alcove behind the Great Hall. From there, one could easily access the dining area without being noticed. If someone wanted to swap the chalice, that would have been the perfect route."

Elise pressed further. "Do you know who might have had knowledge of these tunnels? Who among the reenactors would have been likely to use them?"

Alistair paused, his gaze distant. "I've seen Lady Eleanor near the old passageways more than once. She's taken an interest in the castle's architecture, always asking questions about its history, its defences. She may know about the tunnels. Edwin too—he's often prided himself on being a true lord of Langford, and I suspect he's aware of the tunnels' existence."

"And Marcus, the archer?" Elise asked, recalling his tendency to stay in the background, watching from a distance.

Alistair's expression grew thoughtful. "He may have come across them, yes. Marcus spends a great deal of time in the south wing and near the armoury. He's curious by nature, and I wouldn't be surprised if he's discovered some of the castle's secrets on his own."

Elise's mind raced as she considered the implications. The hidden tunnels allowed the suspects to move without detection, explaining how they could have manipulated the events of the feast with such precision. Each of them had both motive and access, but the tunnels provided them with something even more valuable: the ability to act unseen.

THE POISONED CHALICE

127

"Thank you, Alistair," she said finally, her tone solemn. "You've given me a crucial piece of the puzzle."

Alistair inclined his head, a hint of sadness in his eyes. "I only hope that you can bring peace to Langford, Detective. The castle has borne witness to many tragedies, and it deserves to rest."

With the Keeper's Code in mind, Elise returned to the Great Hall, knowing that the final confrontation was inevitable. She gathered Eleanor, Edwin, and Marcus, each of them tense as they faced her. She spoke, her voice calm but unyielding.

"I know that the three of you had access to the hidden tunnels in Langford Castle. These tunnels gave you the means to carry out a plan, to swap the chalice undetected and orchestrate Gareth's death."

Eleanor lifted her chin, her expression defiant. "Are you suggesting that we used Langford's secrets to commit murder, Detective?"

"Yes, I am," Elise replied bluntly. "The ritual, the altered script, the poisoned chalice—all of it points to a calculated plan to eliminate Gareth, with each of you playing a part. The tunnels allowed you to execute it flawlessly, moving without being seen, using the castle's own shadows to your advantage."

Edwin's face paled, and Marcus looked away, a shadow of regret crossing his face.

"You all had motives," Elise continued, her gaze piercing. "Eleanor, you saw Gareth as a threat to the court's unity. Edwin, you resented his challenges to your authority. And Marcus, you had a personal grudge over his attempts to control the group's funds. You each believed that you were upholding Langford's legacy by removing Gareth."

Eleanor's voice was barely a whisper. "We... we never intended for it to end this way."

"But it did," Elise replied, her tone cold. "The Keeper's Code was meant to protect the castle, not to justify murder. You used its secrets to carry out a twisted form of justice, all in the name of loyalty and honour."

Silence fell over the room as the weight of her words settled on them. Each of them had believed they were acting for the greater good, bound by a legacy that had become a trap, blinding them to the consequences of their actions.

As Elise left the hall, she knew that Langford Castle's secrets would no longer remain in the shadows. The Keeper's Code had been twisted to serve a dark purpose, but now, the truth would finally bring light to the castle's haunted history.

The court of Langford Castle, bound by tradition and betrayal, would face the consequences of their own deeds, no longer able to hide behind masks of loyalty.

Chapter 27: The Lady's Lament

As the investigation drew closer to its conclusion, Elise could feel the weight of Langford Castle's tragic history pressing down on everyone within its walls. But no one seemed more affected than Lady Isolde. She had always carried herself with an air of defiance, masking any vulnerability behind a proud and determined facade. Now, however, Elise found her alone in the gardens, her face streaked with tears as she sat hunched on a stone bench.

Elise approached quietly, sensing that this moment of raw emotion might hold answers that Isolde had kept hidden.

"Lady Isolde," she said softly, her tone gentle but firm. "I know this has been hard on you. But I need to understand what truly happened between you and Gareth."

Isolde looked up, her eyes red and weary. She wiped a tear from her cheek, letting out a shaky breath. "Detective Morrigan... I never wanted things to end this way. Gareth—he wasn't just a part of the reenactment to me. Once, he was... everything."

Elise waited, sensing that Isolde needed to unburden herself. She sat down beside her, giving her space to speak.

"It started out as something beautiful," Isolde continued, her voice barely above a whisper. "Gareth was passionate, intense, and he had this way of making everything feel... real. Like I was truly living the role of Lady Isolde, like I was part of Langford's legacy. But as time went on, I realized he wanted more than just my loyalty. He wanted complete control—over me, over the group, over everything."

Her voice broke slightly, and she took a moment to compose herself. "When I tried to end things with him, he wouldn't accept it. He said I was abandoning him, that I was betraying the 'honour' we'd built together. He even started hinting at things he'd learned about me, things I'd shared with him in confidence."

Elise felt a chill settle over her. "Are you saying he threatened you, Isolde?"

Isolde nodded, her face twisted with regret. "Yes. He said he'd tell the others that I'd betrayed him, that I wasn't loyal to the court's traditions. He knew how much this group, this role, meant to me, and he used it against me. He threatened to ruin me, to turn everyone against me if I didn't... if I didn't give in to his demands."

"What kind of demands?" Elise asked, her tone gentle but insistent.

Isolde's gaze dropped, her hands trembling as she clutched them tightly together. "He wanted me to support him unconditionally, to back every decision he made within the court. He wanted me to speak out against Edwin, to rally others to his side. And when I refused, he became... relentless."

She paused, her voice breaking. "Gareth made me feel like I had no way out. He said he would make everyone see me as a traitor, that he'd ruin my reputation and expose every secret I'd ever trusted him with. I was terrified, Detective. I thought... I thought there was nothing I could do to stop him."

Elise placed a comforting hand on her shoulder, her voice soft. "So, what did you do, Isolde?"

Isolde swallowed, her gaze distant. "I spoke to Eleanor. I told her what Gareth was doing, how he'd turned into this... this tyrant, demanding loyalty while using fear to keep everyone in line. She told me she'd help me, that she'd find a way to make him understand that he couldn't control us. I thought she meant she'd confront him, force him to see reason. But then, Eleanor started planning the ritual, the 'Traitor's Trial,' and I realized that she intended to make an example of him."

"And you went along with it?" Elise asked quietly, not accusing, but urging her to face the truth.

Isolde nodded, shame clouding her expression. "Yes. I thought the ritual would force him to confront his own behaviour, to see how

THE POISONED CHALICE   131

far he'd strayed from the ideals he claimed to hold. But then... then Eleanor mentioned the chalice. She said that it would be a symbolic punishment, that Gareth would drink from it and understand that he wasn't untouchable."

A shiver ran through Elise. "Did you know the chalice was poisoned?"

"No," Isolde replied quickly, her voice filled with desperation. "I swear, I didn't know. I thought it was just meant to scare him, to make him think twice before threatening anyone again. I thought he'd take the hint, that we'd all move on."

"But someone decided to take it further," Elise said, piecing it together. "Someone knew about the poisoned chalice and used that opportunity to eliminate Gareth."

Isolde nodded, guilt heavy in her eyes. "I didn't want him dead, Detective. I just wanted him to stop. I thought... I thought that by helping Eleanor, I could protect myself, protect the group."

Elise felt a pang of sympathy as she looked at Isolde's tear-streaked face. "In trying to protect yourself, you became part of something far darker. You allowed Eleanor to manipulate events, to use Gareth's own threats against him. And in the end, his obsession with loyalty and betrayal became a self-fulfilling prophecy."

Isolde's voice was barely audible. "Yes. I see that now."

Elise took a deep breath, letting the silence settle between them for a moment. "Thank you for telling me, Isolde. I know this hasn't been easy."

Isolde looked away, a tear sliding down her cheek. "Nothing about this has been easy, Detective. I loved Gareth once, but he became someone I didn't recognize. And now... now I have to live with what's happened."

Elise nodded, understanding that the weight of Gareth's death would haunt Isolde—and everyone involved—for a long time. The twisted loyalties, the manipulation, the tragic end to a once-promising love—all of it had spiralled out of control, leading to a death cloaked in shadows and betrayal.

As Elise left Isolde in the garden, she knew that this final revelation had brought her closer to understanding the true heart of Langford Castle's tragedy. Gareth's threats, his attempts to control and intimidate, had driven those around him to desperate measures. The court, bound by loyalty and tradition, had fractured under the weight of secrets, each member pushed to act out of fear, love, or revenge.

The castle's ancient walls had borne witness to a drama as old as the stones themselves—a tale of passion, betrayal, and the devastating consequences of power left unchecked.

And now, with the last of the secrets laid bare, Elise knew she would finally bring Langford Castle's haunted legacy to an end.

Chapter 28: The Poisoner's Apprentice

Just when Elise thought she had unearthed every secret within Langford Castle, a new confession cast fresh doubt on the story. This time, it came from an unexpected source: a younger member of the reenactment group, a quiet, observant figure named Alice, who had often stayed on the edges of the action, meticulously taking notes and learning the ways of historical herbs and apothecary techniques.

Elise found Alice in the small apothecary room the group used for preparing herbal remedies and potions for the reenactments. Alice looked up as Elise entered, her eyes wide, a mixture of nerves and excitement flashing across her face.

"Detective Morrigan," she greeted, glancing down at the bundles of herbs and bottles of liquids arranged neatly on the table. "Is there something I can help you with?"

"Yes, Alice," Elise replied, her tone steady but probing. "I understand you've taken an interest in historical herbs and poisons as part of the reenactment. I'd like to know more about that—about what you've learned and practiced."

Alice's cheeks flushed, and she fidgeted with a sprig of dried lavender. "I—I have been experimenting with herbs, yes. But only for accuracy, Detective. It's part of my role as an apothecary, you see. I wanted everything to be as authentic as possible. I've studied old manuscripts, learned the effects of different plants... I even helped prepare some of the 'remedies' we used during the reenactments."

Elise nodded, watching her carefully. "Alice, did you ever experiment with more dangerous substances? Something that could be used to harm someone?"

Alice's face paled slightly, and she looked away, her fingers twisting together. "I... I may have tried some of the stronger herbs. For research, of course," she added quickly, her tone defensive. "I wanted to understand how they worked, what the historical effects would have been. But I swear, Detective, it was never with any bad intentions."

"Which herbs, specifically?" Elise pressed, her tone gentle but firm.

Alice took a shaky breath, casting a glance at the shelves behind her. "Well, there's belladonna... it's a powerful sedative and can be deadly in high doses. And hemlock, which was historically used as a poison. I read about them in some of the old texts we keep in the castle library. They were just part of the historical record, you know? I thought understanding them would make my role more believable."

"And did anyone else know about your 'experiments'?" Elise asked, watching her reaction closely.

Alice hesitated, then nodded. "Lady Eleanor knew. She found me once, preparing a tincture, and she seemed... impressed, I suppose. She said I had a natural talent for the apothecary's craft. After that, she started asking me to help with certain... preparations."

Elise's eyebrows rose. "What kind of preparations, Alice?"

"Mostly harmless things—herbal infusions, teas to help with focus or relaxation before the reenactments," Alice explained quickly. "But a few weeks before the feast, she asked me to prepare something special, something that would evoke the 'power' of Langford's legacy. She didn't give me specifics, but she hinted that it should carry... a sense of fear, something that would remind people of the consequences of betrayal."

Elise felt a chill as she processed Alice's words. "Did she ask you to make something with a poisonous effect?"

Alice swallowed, her eyes widening with guilt. "Not directly, but she asked me to prepare an infusion with belladonna and a touch of hemlock. I thought she just wanted it for show, something to heighten the drama of the ritual. I prepared a very diluted mixture, something that would give a bitter taste but wouldn't actually cause harm if only a small amount was used."

THE POISONED CHALICE   135

Elise's heart raced as she realized the implications. "And what happened to that mixture, Alice? Did you give it to Eleanor?"

Alice nodded, wringing her hands. "Yes, I gave it to her the night before the feast. She said she would add it to the chalice to create a sense of 'danger' during the Traitor's Trial. I didn't know she would use it on Gareth. I thought it was just for show, to make the ritual feel real. I never meant for anyone to die."

Elise's voice was calm but unyielding. "But someone took that mixture and turned it into a lethal dose. Whether it was Eleanor or someone else, the belladonna and hemlock you prepared became a weapon."

Alice's face crumpled, and she looked down, her hands shaking. "I... I didn't mean for this to happen, Detective. I was just trying to be accurate, to bring history to life. I never thought anyone would actually use it to... to kill."

Elise placed a hand on Alice's shoulder, her voice gentle. "I believe you, Alice. But your work—the herbs, the knowledge—was manipulated by someone else to achieve their own ends. You may not have intended to harm, but your talents became a part of this tragedy."

Alice sniffled, her voice trembling. "I trusted Eleanor. I thought she wanted to honour Langford's history, not twist it into... into murder."

Elise nodded, feeling a mix of pity and resolve. "Eleanor took advantage of your skills, Alice, using you as a means to carry out her vision of justice. She played on your dedication, your desire for authenticity, and turned it into something dark."

As she left Alice in the apothecary room, Elise knew this was the final piece of the puzzle. Eleanor had orchestrated every part of the ritual, manipulating each person around her—Isolde with her fears, Marcus with his grudge, Edwin with his loyalty, and Alice with her knowledge of herbs and poisons.

Langford Castle's twisted reenactment had been a deadly drama with Eleanor as its mastermind, using history as a mask for her own desire to control and punish. And with Alice's reluctant confession, the truth had finally come to light.

Chapter 29: A Web of Lies

The secrets of Langford Castle had finally unravelled, but Elise knew that one final confrontation remained. She had all the pieces—the betrayals, the rivalries, the hidden motives, and the deadly plot to turn Gareth into the sacrificial traitor. It was time to confront the remaining suspects and reveal the true mastermind behind the poisoned chalice.

Gathering the key members in the Great Hall—Eleanor, Edwin, Marcus, Isolde, and Alice—Elise could feel the tension in the room. Each face reflected a mixture of fear, regret, and defiance. They were caught in a web of their own lies, but Elise was ready to reveal the truth.

She took a deep breath and began, her voice calm but unyielding. "Each of you had a part in Gareth's death, whether by action or silence. Over the past days, I've pieced together the events that led to his poisoning, and I can now say with certainty who orchestrated this murder."

The group looked at one another, uneasy, as Elise continued.

"Let's start with you, Edwin." She turned to the self-appointed "lord" of Langford, who looked back at her with a hardened gaze. "You resented Gareth's challenges to your authority, saw his ambition as a threat to your position. When Eleanor suggested the ritual to remind him of his place, you agreed, thinking it would restore order."

Edwin's jaw clenched, but he said nothing.

"And Isolde," Elise went on, her gaze softening slightly. "You were once close to Gareth. You trusted him, confided in him. But when he turned possessive, using your secrets as leverage, you were desperate to escape his control. When Eleanor suggested casting him as the traitor, you went along with it, believing it would give you the distance you needed."

Isolde looked down, her expression filled with regret.

"Marcus," Elise said, turning to the archer, whose face was pale. "You wanted to protect the group's resources from Gareth's reckless plans. You felt he would drain Langford's resources for his own ends. You supported the idea of a ritualized punishment, hoping it would make Gareth understand he wasn't the sole authority."

Marcus gave a small nod, his face drawn with shame.

"And then there's Alice," Elise continued, looking at the young woman who had unwittingly played a pivotal role. "You wanted to honour the past, to add historical accuracy to your role. But Eleanor took advantage of your knowledge, asking you to prepare a mixture with belladonna and hemlock, hinting that it was just for the 'drama' of the ritual. She knew exactly what she was doing, and she used you to make it possible."

Alice swallowed, looking away, tears brimming in her eyes.

Finally, Elise turned to Eleanor, her voice dropping to a cold, unwavering tone. "And you, Eleanor. The 'queen' of Langford. You orchestrated every part of this plan, weaving together everyone's grievances into a single scheme to eliminate Gareth. You cast him as the traitor, using their fears and resentments to justify his punishment. You manipulated Alice into preparing a poison you could use, disguising it as tradition. You played each of them, exploiting their trust in you."

Eleanor's face was stony, but there was a faint glimmer of defiance in her eyes.

"You used Langford's history, its rituals, and its secrets as tools to get what you wanted," Elise pressed. "You made Gareth's death seem like the inevitable result of his own actions. You even led Alice to believe it was just a harmless concoction, all for the sake of adding 'realism' to the ritual. But in reality, you were orchestrating his murder from the start."

Eleanor's calm facade finally cracked, and she looked around the room, her gaze lingering on each of the people she had so meticulously controlled.

"He would have destroyed everything," she said quietly, her voice tinged with desperation. "Gareth was reckless, obsessive. He didn't

THE POISONED CHALICE 139

understand what it meant to preserve Langford's legacy. I did what was necessary. I protected the court."

Elise shook her head, her voice cutting through the silence. "You didn't protect the court, Eleanor. You destroyed it. You used loyalty and honour as a mask for your ambition, turning everyone against Gareth because he threatened your control. But in the end, it wasn't about tradition—it was about power."

The room was silent as her words settled, each of the reenactors absorbing the truth. Eleanor had been the mastermind, using each of their fears and desires to her advantage, weaving a web of lies that had ensnared them all.

Edwin looked at Eleanor, anger flashing in his eyes. "We trusted you. You led us to believe this was for Langford's honour. But it was all just a game to you, wasn't it?"

Eleanor's gaze hardened. "It wasn't a game, Edwin. It was survival. Gareth would have destroyed everything we built."

Isolde's voice was barely a whisper. "You used me. You told me it was for the good of the court, that I was protecting myself... but you were only protecting yourself."

Alice, her face stricken, finally spoke, her voice trembling. "You made me believe it was for history, for accuracy. I didn't know I was... that I was making poison."

Eleanor met Elise's gaze one last time, her face a mask of resigned defiance. "You can judge me however you like, Detective. But everything I did, I did for Langford. You'll never understand what it means to be part of something this important."

Elise's voice was calm but firm. "I understand perfectly, Eleanor. You sacrificed a man's life to protect your own version of Langford's legacy. But that's not honour—it's corruption. And now, the truth will see the light."

With that final word, Elise knew the case was closed. Eleanor had manipulated the court, weaving a web of lies and betrayals to achieve her goals, and in doing so, had torn apart the very group she claimed to protect.

As the reenactors dispersed, each of them grappling with the truth, Elise felt a strange sense of resolution. Langford Castle's secrets had finally been revealed, its legacy exposed as a shadowed tale of ambition, betrayal, and tragic consequences.

The web of lies was finally broken, and with it, Langford's haunted history could finally be laid to rest.

Chapter 30: The Last Toast

The case was finally closed. The labyrinthine secrets, the betrayals, and the calculated murder had all come to light, leaving Langford Castle stripped of its illusions and shadows. As Elise stood alone in the Great Hall, the ancient walls seemed to breathe a sigh of relief, as if even they were weary from the weight of so many secrets.

She looked around the grand room, now eerily silent. Only hours ago, it had been filled with the voices of those who had played their parts in Gareth's death. Now, it was empty, the echoes of their final confrontation lingering like whispers caught in the stone.

On the long banquet table sat a single chalice, an untouched silver goblet with delicate, intricate engravings that shimmered faintly in the dim light. Elise approached it slowly, her mind heavy with the memories of the events that had transpired. She picked up the chalice, its cool weight grounding her as she looked into its depths. The cup was empty, yet it felt as if it were filled with the memories of every betrayal, every manipulation, every twisted motive that had culminated in Gareth's death.

This chalice was a symbol—a symbol of honour corrupted, of loyalty turned to poison, of history wielded as a weapon. In the name of tradition, Lady Eleanor had sacrificed everything she claimed to hold dear, leading each member of the court into a deadly game that none could escape unscathed.

Elise lifted the chalice, holding it aloft as if in a silent toast. She could almost hear the echoes of past banquets, feel the weight of centuries of ambition, rivalry, and dark secrets lingering in the air.

"To Langford Castle," she murmured softly, her voice reverberating through the hall. "To its shadows and stories, to those who believed in loyalty and those who twisted it."

She lowered the chalice, gazing into its depths. "And to those who paid the price for it."

For a moment, she closed her eyes, letting the silence wash over her. She could feel the spirit of the place—its dark history, the lives it had touched and taken, the tragedies it had witnessed. It was a place of haunting beauty, but also of shadows that had grown too deep, too entwined in the people who tried to preserve it.

Elise placed the chalice back on the table, untouched and untarnished, leaving it as a silent testament to the twisted drama that had unfolded. She knew that Langford's secrets would linger here, woven into the castle's history, but they would no longer hold power over those who sought to honour them.

As she turned to leave the hall, Elise glanced back one last time, the empty chalice glinting softly in the dim light, a final reminder of the cost of loyalty twisted into obsession. Langford Castle had given up its ghosts, and as she stepped through its doors, she felt that, at last, its history might finally be at peace.

Disclaimer

This book is a work of fiction, and all characters, events, and locations are products of the author's imagination or are used fictitiously only.

The Poisoned Chalice is a fictional story created solely for entertainment purposes. Any resemblance to real persons, living or dead, or actual events, is purely coincidental. The reenactment setting, while inspired by historical and modern traditions, is fictionalized and does not depict any actual reenactment groups, events, or individuals. Additionally, no historical figures or real-world organizations should be inferred to have influenced this narrative, nor does this work intend to represent medieval reenactment communities in general. The book includes elements of mystery and crime that are not meant to reflect or imply any real-life occurrences.